THE URBANA FREE LIBRARY
W9-BDU-342

GENERAL ESCOBAR'S WAR

JOSÉ LUIS OLAIZOLA

General Escobar's War

Translated by Richard Goodyear

IGNATIUS PRESS SAN FRANCISCO

Original Spanish edition:
La guerra del general Escobar
Editorial Planeta, Barcelona, Spain

Cover photo:
A Trumpeter of the Civil Guards (c. 1900)
Jack Benton/Archive Photos/Getty Images

Cover design by John Herreid

ISBN 978-1-62164-052-3
Library of Congress Control Number 2015948591
Printed in the United States of America ♾

To Alfredo Escobar,
the general's nephew,
whose constant encouragement
has made this book possible

CONTENTS

TRANSLATOR'S INTRODUCTION

Many Spaniards did not have an opportunity to choose sides in the civil war that is described in this book—the Civil War, to accord its name the capitalization in which it is usually clothed. That choice was often dictated to them by chance, according to which side of the conflict controlled the territory in which they found themselves when the war broke out on the night of July 17, 1936. Many who fought in it were forced to do so, dragooned into serving by whichever side ruled the spot on the map where, by sheer geographical accident, they happened to be when they woke up the next morning.

That was not the case for Antonio Escobar Huertas. That morning he was in Barcelona, where the republican government was in control. But the decision he made to fight on the republican side had nothing to do with geography. Nor, more importantly, did he make the choice he did because he agreed or sympathized with the ideology, goals, and conduct of the Republic. He disagreed with them in very significant respects—some of them fundamental. He fought for the Republic because, as a deeply conservative and devoutly Catholic colonel in the Civil Guard, he felt himself bound by the oath he had sworn before God to uphold and serve the legally constituted government.

The roots of the military revolt that erupted that July night were centuries old, nourished by the blood spilled in the many wars waged by, against, and in Spain throughout its history. The longest of those wars extended over almost eight hundred years, from the Ummayad Arab invasion in 711 to the spread by 718 of Muslim rule over almost all of what is Spain today, through the culmination of the *Reconquista*'s reclamation of Spain for Christianity, piece by hard-won piece, in the fall of Granada in 1492 to King Ferdinand II and Queen Isabella I.

But Spain was to be at war off and on, in whole or in part, for almost 450 years more: local rebellions, colonial wars to build its far-flung empire and then to try (unsuccessfully) to preserve it, a thirteen-year war of succession, a war of independence with Napoleonic France, a disastrous war with the United States, and civil wars—most notably those known as the three Carlist Wars (1833–1839, 1846–1849, 1872–1876), which were fought over the disputed succession to the throne of the Bourbon Queen Isabella II. This legacy of conflict, often marked by no-holds-barred violence, asserted itself (literally with a vengeance) in the Civil War.

But even when the multi-faceted rifts in Spanish society did not result in outright war, they still destabilized Spanish politics and society in general. By one count there were thirty-seven coups, twelve of them successful, between 1814 and 1874. Isabella II was overthrown in 1868 and replaced by King Amedeo I, who in turn abdicated under pressure in 1873 and was succeeded by the First Republic, which then gave way to the restoration of the Bourbons in 1874. Prime Minister Antonio Cánovas was assassinated in 1897 by an Italian anarchist. In 1909, Barcelona was the scene of a "Tragic Week" of political, class, and intensely anticlerical violence, leaving nearly three hundred dead (five by firing squad) and sowing the seeds of a deep bitterness that would be reaped in the Civil War.

The 1920s brought the colonial Rif War, fought in what is today Morocco and marked by a particularly disastrous battle at Annual that many blamed on King Alfonso XIII. A coup in 1923 that the military did not oppose and Alfonso supported ushered in the dictatorship of Miguel Primo de Rivera, who would then be ushered out in 1930, when he lost their support. Less than fifteen months later it was Alfonso's turn to be ushered out, after the municipal elections of April 12, 1931—which were regarded as a referendum on the monarchy—yielded a result that made his position untenable. He left Spain (though he did not abdicate until 1941), and the Second Republic was proclaimed two days later.

But the Republic was no cure-all. Amid growing turmoil—riots, violent strikes and suppressions of strikes, attempted coups, widespread attacks on churches, convents, and clergy, deadly set-tos between the authorities and disaffected groups of citizens, street shoot-outs between opposing factions, a mounting wave of political assassinations—many concluded that the republican government was incapable of fulfilling its most basic responsibility of maintaining order. The failure of the government to provide security convinced many in the military that they were discharged from their sworn obligation to uphold the Republic, that in fact they had a higher obligation:

to overthrow it. In August 1932, General Sanjurjo headed a coup attempt that failed miserably. But conspiracies simmered on, ultimately boiling over in the uprising that sparked the Civil War.

Internecine strife dogged both the nationalists and the republicans. One of the nationalist factions was the Falange, a political movement (founded by Miguel Primo de Rivera's son José Antonio) that has particular importance in this book because General Escobar's son José was a committed member of it. Other nationalist factions included CEDA, a Catholic and anti-Communist political party that competed with the Falange for members and influence, and two groups dedicated to upholding the monarchy—but in the name of two different lines of royal descent: the Carlists and, supporting the Bourbon line, the Alfonsists. The nationalist commander, Generalísimo Francisco Franco, succeeded in welding these groups together by merging them all in the Falange, renaming the resulting entity the National Movement.

Lacking a leader who had the personal prestige that Franco enjoyed among his followers (and the added advantage of being at the top of both the military and the political chains of command; he was formally recognized by the nationalist generals as the chief of the Spanish state during the eleventh week of the war), the Republic never achieved the unity that the nationalists attained. The Socialists, anarchists, anarcho-syndicalists, and Communists were particularly powerful in the government of the Republic and passionately committed to defeating the nationalists. But they contended fiercely with each other from beginning to end, often with predictably negative effects on the war effort. And, except for the Communists, they had an ideological antipathy to military discipline, which forced the Republic to rely on militias and reduced the number of disciplined combat units it was able to field. Franco did not have to deal with such problems.

La guerra del general Escobar was published by Planeta in an edition of 180,000 copies, and awarded the Planeta prize for a novel, in 1983. It instantly caused an uproar. Franco had died in 1975 after thirty-six years as dictator of Spain (not counting the three Civil War years), and the transition to democracy had begun in a constitution adopted in 1978, but memories of the Civil War were fresh and its wounds were still open. Veterans and others on both sides of the conflict found a good deal to object to in this highly sympathetic portrait of a devoutly Catholic soldier who, on the one hand, adhered to his principles by fighting against those who were intent on overthrowing the Republic, but who on the other also viewed with deep distaste and sorrow the political radicalism and hatred of religion among those who fought to uphold the Republic.

The author of the book, José Luis Olaizola, is himself a devout Catholic and far from a political radical. Yet he proposed its protagonist to his fellow Spaniards as a nuanced exemplar worthy of emulation, and as an aid to healing and going forward together into a future that would never see again the waste, misery, and tragedy wrought by the Civil War.

He and his book were widely praised when it was published. But they were also attacked, at least on one occasion (when Olaizola had to make his escape from a lecture hall through a back door) with the threat of violence. Civil wars have long tails, as anyone who has studied American history will know, and the Spanish Civil War was not exceptional in that respect.

Indeed, it wasn't particularly exceptional in any respect, other than in the sense of Tolstoy's dictum that each unhappy family is unhappy in its own way. Rather, in its clash of ideologies, lies, and egos; its brutality; and its tragically harsh light on the human condition, it was a paradigm of civil wars generally—including the European civil wars we call World Wars I and II (from both of which Spain largely kept its distance, and for the second of which, largely because of the participation of Germany, Italy, and the Soviet Union, the Civil War is often described as a rehearsal).

Anyone touched by civil war can learn from *La guerra del general Escobar*. I am very grateful, particularly to its author, for the opportunity to make it available in English. I thank Antonio Gordillo Fernández de Villavicencio for bringing it to my attention. And I dedicate my translation, in all admiration, to the memory of Antonio Escobar Huertas, to José Luis Olaizola, and to my wife, Carmen Echavarren Ruedas.

Richard Goodyear

AUTHOR'S PREFACE

Don Antonio Escobar Huertas, a colonel of the Civil Guard on July 19, 1936, director general of security of Catalonia during the May Days of 1937, and general-in-chief of the Army of Extremadura from October 1938 until the end of the Spanish Civil War, continues to be, for the Spanish army, no more than a sergeant who enlisted as a volunteer, for an indefinite period and without pay, when he was sixteen years and one day old.

If the curious historian requests General Escobar's file from the General Military Archive of Segovia—where the personnel files of all Spanish soldiers are kept—he will be shown a small file with the legend, in pencil: "Sergeant".

The narrator—who is no historian—in the belief that the foregoing is a subterfuge that will serve no good purpose, embarked on a reconstruction of his story. In doing so, he has had the benefit of personal memories of the general, thanks to the incalculable help of the following:

Alfredo Escobar, the general's nephew
Antonio Escobar Valtierra, the general's son
Féliz Villaverde, the general's nephew
Pedro Masips, the general's captain adjutant

The reconstruction of the general's military career has been made possible thanks to Ramón Salas Larrazábal's monumental work, *History of the People's Army of the Republic.*

The studies published by Luis Romero, Ramón Garriga, Cristóbal Zaragoza, and Juan Antonio Pérez Mateos have also been of great assistance.

The author may have committed some anachronisms, even deliberately, but he has taken care that any event carrying implications for the honor or veracity of historical persons would withstand documentary scrutiny.

This book is not an account of a war, but rather an account of a man who lived a war.

It is not a work of history but a novel, in order to soften the sadness and even the cruelty of what happened, because it is well known that novels are works of fiction. If only what is recounted had been fiction.

José Luis Olaizola

GENERAL ESCOBAR'S WAR

THE PROSECUTOR in my court-martial here in this castle and prison, Montjuich, accuses me of the crime of high treason in very simple terms. But, during the trial itself, he's elaborated on that accusation with this refinement: "In my judgment, a soldier in this war who calls himself a Catholic has been a traitor twice over: to his Fatherland and to his God."

This drew an admonition from the presiding military judge: "Confine yourself to the referral of charges. Colonel Escobar's on trial not for his religious convictions but for rising up in arms against the regime that won the war and that all civilized nations have recognized as the legitimate government."

Even though I was the general-in-chief of the Army of Extremadura when the war ended, I'm being tried as a colonel because the winners of the war still see me as the colonel of the Civil Guard who in July 1936—here in this city of Barcelona, as it happens—fought against the rebel soldiers who stopped being rebels when they won the war. My defense counsel explained it to me this way: "Bear in mind, Colonel, that the rebellion's been redeemed by victory."

The prosecutor accepted the presiding judge's admonition respectfully, but he deftly turned his apology to good use by making an allegation that pained me very much: "My comment slipped out, Mr. President, because of the acts of the accused on the night of July 19 and 20, 1936, in the Carmelite convent on Calle Lauria in this city, as a result of which twenty-five loyal officers, and a number of monks that has not been determined but exceeded fifty, were murdered."

I got the impression the members of the court-martial were glad to hear this allegation, not because those poor people died but as a justification for the sentence the court has to hand down.

Although I've been in solitary confinement for seven months in this cell, rumors do reach me. My fellow officer-prisoners say Franco himself worked out the blueprint for the sentences to be imposed. The role of the courts-martial is just to follow it in specific cases. If that's so, there's no way at all for me to be cleared of responsibility for anything and everything that happened in the convent on Calle Lauria. It was very complicated, very traumatic.

I was taken aback by the allegation, or at least I hadn't expected it, because my lawyer has emphasized to me that the truly serious charge we're up against is that I didn't join the National Movement on July 19, 1936.

~

I first heard about what's now called the Movement in a telephone call from my brother Alfredo, who was calling from Madrid. He was a lieutenant colonel of the Civil Guard on July 18, in the Urban Division, but he had contacts in the press office.

He told me the Army of Africa had staged an uprising. Although it didn't occur to me then, I think now that the reason he called me, his considerably older brother (by seven years), might have been to find out what position I was thinking of taking. Our oldest brother is Ramón, who is also a colonel of the Civil Guard, but fortunately for him he had already retired at the time of the uprising. My son Antonio is a member of the Civil Guard, too, with the rank of captain.

Alfredo warned me that members of the Falange had been involved in the African rebellion, which was what upset me most because my youngest son, José, nineteen years old, was a very active Falangist. I remember that my son Antonio, the captain, took a very dim view of that and found fault with me over it: "Why do you accept José's messing around in politics, Father?"

I didn't know what to say, and he persisted: "The Escobars have never messed around in politics."

"You're right, son, we've always messed around in the Civil Guard."

When I don't know what to say, either I act as though I'm deaf—which is fair enough because I can't hear anything through my right ear—or I make my getaway with a joke.

But Antonio was right. What José was doing worried me because the Falange was at that point an underground party, in which he headed a company of a hundred men. It seemed impossible to me that José should be the head of anything. I still thought of him as a child, maybe because when I was widowed he seemed like more of an orphan than my other two children. Antonio was already married to Angelita, and my daughter, Emilia, was about to take her vows in the order of the Sisters of Adoration. My older son also disapproved of that. He thought Emilia should take care of me in my widowerhood rather than go into a convent.

I've sometimes had my differences with my son Antonio. He would occasionally let his arrogance show, maybe because his background isn't the same as mine. I was a sergeant at the Civil Guard's Officer Candidate School in Getafe, whereas he studied at the Infantry Academy in Toledo. He stood out there as a horseman and a fencer and was a sergeant of honor.

Antonio is also waiting to be tried in this same castle, Montjuich. What a coincidence. A sad one, because they don't let us see each other.

~

My brother Alfredo was a classmate of Franco's at the Infantry Academy in Toledo. My brother Ramón and I, on the other hand, following my father's advice, enlisted in the Civil Guard as volunteers, for an indefinite period and without pay. This earned us the opportunity to go to the Civil Guard's Officer Candidate School, where our applications were given preference because our father had died in battle, during the War of 1898, at Santiago de Cuba. He had attained the rank of major. We were able to make it possible for our brother Alfredo to go to the Infantry Academy, which meant he started his career as an officer.

When Alfredo called me that afternoon of July 18, he didn't know Franco was at the head of the uprising in Africa. That came out later. What he did tell me was that the "director" of the uprising, at least on the peninsula, was Brigadier General Emilio Mola, who was posted in Pamplona. His link with the Movement in Catalonia was his brother Ramón, who was on garrison duty in Barcelona with the rank of captain.

Mola laid down the guiding principle of the uprising in a communiqué in which, echoing a phrase from the Gospel, he warned that anybody who wasn't with him would be against him, and that the victors would take no pity on any comrades who didn't fulfill their obligations as such.

We didn't know all this until later. Nor did we know on that afternoon of July 18 that the revolt in Africa was irreversible: when it was just a few hours old and we knew almost nothing about it on the peninsula, the rebels had already shot the military commander in Melilla, General Romerales, along with various other commanders and officers who couldn't see their way clear to comradeship as General Mola's communiqué defined it.

In my solitude now, which I share only with the patch of blue sky that I can see through my cell window—a pale blue because winter has arrived—I read whatever I can get my hands on. The commandant of the fort is kind about this and usually brings me magazines himself. "Here, Colonel, read these."

He looks at me compassionately on account of what might lie in store for me, but above all for the sad fact that a man like me should have been so mistaken during the war. The magazines are those of the winning side, of course, and I sometimes think the commandant makes them available to me so I will think over what I read in them and have a change of heart—repent so contritely that my bleak prospects in the court-martial will improve.

A vain illusion. One of these magazines glorifies General Mola, who also warned in 1936 that the rebellion was not going to be an old-fashioned coup or pronunciamento, in which the rebels would take over the central telephone exchange in Madrid and give orders from there. No, the rebellion would have to prevail in each and every garrison in Spain, because this time there would be nothing but unconditional surrender and a crushing, definitive victory. Although I still don't think Franco was too involved in planning the uprising, it has taken on his spirit with impressive thoroughness. I'm talking about unconditional surrender, and about the relentlessness toward those of us who haven't acted as true comrades would. If he has been so merciless to so many so far, he is not going to make an exception for me.

I had dealings with General Mola when he was director general of security and the Corps had a reporting relationship of sorts to him. I remember him as a man of great bureaucratic nicety, which I thought was good because I've always felt this country was very disorderly. He was not likeable. Nor do I remember him as being a particularly fervent person religiously, so I was very surprised when I heard he had promised to raise the cross of Christ, at the head of his Carlists, during the battle for Madrid in November 1936. We certainly needed Christ in our capital city during those days, but the way Mola proposed to bring him in didn't strike me as very fitting. Being a Catholic is now part of the regime's organic principles, but when the chaplain arranged the other day for me to go to the Mass they celebrate here every morning at eight, I was surprised to see there were just two of us there. The other was a soldier who intends to go to seminary as soon as he's discharged from the army. The boy looked at me disapprovingly. He reminded me of my son José. Any young man of twenty or so reminds me of José.

Mola's brother Ramón resembled him. He had the same worried look, but unlike the general he didn't wear glasses. When the uprising failed in Barcelona—which was my fault, they now say—the poor young man committed suicide. What a terrible thing. I recall seeing him walking along the rambla with his wife and a little boy.

I remember very clearly everybody I've ever known, because I make up for being slightly deaf by focusing closely on people. My deafness varies from day to day and is at its worst when it's humid. But anyway, I'm not as deaf as people think. Also, by paying careful attention, I've learned to read lips. I say all this because anybody who wants to fool me has to do it behind my back. And I say it because I've seen there are people who don't remember me but whom I do remember. Even if they aren't in the Civil Guard, I haven't come across many soldiers whose rank and posting I can't remember, along with when we met.

This has helped me quite a bit in my work in the Corps. As a Civil Guard, you have to know how to read a person as a whole: face, lips, and bearing. Especially if you decide not to get at the truth by beating it out. I made that decision the day I slapped a poacher when I was posted in the town of Fuencarral, near the El Pardo mountains, in Madrid province.

When on July 18 I told my general about the conversation I'd had with Alfredo, he said, "Yes, I know, Escobar. Escofet told me. Do you think it'll be serious?"

It was an idle question. As though he was just thinking out loud, because at that stage nobody in Spain knew what was going to happen. I do remember saying to him, "I don't know, General, but one thing that's clear is that we better nip it in the bud."

I was speaking from what I had learned as a Civil Guard. It's easy to cut off any disturbance or demonstration when it's just begun. But if you let it go on and the confusion grows, it gets out of hand and inevitably ends in bloodshed.

General Aranguren answered, "Of course, of course. You're right."

That's what his lips said, but I could see a deep uneasiness in his eyes. This is what I meant before when I said you have to read a person as a whole.

"Escobar, it's going to be a very hard thing to fight against our comrades."

I think he said it then and more than once afterward, in the days that followed that terrible day. Although he had been a general in the Corps for some time, Aranguren came from the army, and he seemed to have the sense of comradeship that I think Mola was exploiting.

For me, it was always a very hard thing to fight against anybody. I loved order as a positive good, as a way of avoiding a fight. I now love it as a dream.

All of us went through a very bad time, but it was worse for General Aranguren than for anybody else because he did his duty with a broken heart. President Azaña has unfairly said the general sleepwalked through the whole war. He said it to me more than once, and I argued with him about it; but the president was a man of very strong likes and dislikes, and all the deference he showed me turned into criticisms when it came to my general.

In Pedralbes Palace, in January 1937, he said to me, "Don't kid yourself, Escobar, the only thing Aranguren has over you is the way he wears the uniform."

He said it with a laugh, as a joke, because the general and I were known as the best-turned-out commanders in the Corps, and we even seemed to be competing with each other. What childish silliness. The dress uniform of the Civil Guard—dark blue trimmed with gold, with braid on the three-cornered hat—was the most beautiful military uniform in Spain. When we had to wear it for some ceremonial event, Aranguren and I would inspect each other out of the corner of our eye and he would say to me, "Wow, Escobar, you look very elegant."

I would answer, "It's the uniform, General. Hasn't Your Excellency looked at himself in the mirror?"

"No, my assistant dressed me."

Those were good days. I was a little taller than the general, but he had a more aristocratic way about him.

~

President Companys called me to the Palace of the Generalitat that afternoon. It had been very hot in the morning, but a sea breeze came up at noon, and it wove its way from the balcony into the shade of the president's office. The president asked me to sit down with exaggerated friendliness. He was one of the people who shouted when he spoke to me because he thought I was very deaf. So I wouldn't misunderstand the shouting, he maintained an unmistakably forced smile. He explained again about the uprising in Africa, but he brushed it off because Africa was far, far away, farther even than the rest of Spain. He gave the impression that any incident in Africa might take centuries to have an impact on Catalonia.

But he said, "Anyway, Colonel, we'd better take some action." He also reminded me that under the Generalitat's agreements with the central government, public order was the Generalitat's responsibility, so the Civil Guard was, too.

That's the trouble with politicians. They say things over and over again, to the point where you get the impression they are not convinced by what they are saying. I already knew I reported to the Generalitat, from the day I was made colonel of the Urban Division, and he didn't need to remind me. Maybe I didn't take it very cheerfully, or I confused him by asking, "Have you spoken to General Aranguren?"

"Aranguren's been informed," he answered, with no details, "but you're the one who'll be in direct command of the Guards that'll need to get involved in whatever trouble we have to cope with."

I wasn't trying to give an impression of uncertainty by falling back on my supposed deafness, or pretending to be deafer than I was. I just didn't know how to react to this brisk reminder about the obligations of the servants of public order.

I know President Companys wasn't pleased by this conversation, and I wasn't, either, because I would have preferred that he talk directly with my general.

In any case, I was now very concerned and went home to change into civilian clothes. If Companys had found out I had taken off my uniform just then, he certainly would have thought the worst. I asked the maid, who was from Galicia, about my son José, and she told me he hadn't come home to eat but had called to tell her he wasn't coming.

I started to feel a kind of prickling in and around my heart—a shooting pain and a tingling sensation of pins and needles, which starts in my chest and runs along the length of my whole left arm right down to my fingertips. They say it's a symptom experienced by people who die of a heart attack. But that doesn't seem to be the kind of death awaiting me.

I changed out of uniform to go to the Franciscans' church, or what used to be their church, on the rambla. The rambla was beautiful, and the breeze coming up from the harbor seemed to bring with it a spring afternoon. Besides, in civilian clothes I didn't feel the heat so much. If you button the collar of the Corps uniform the way you should, it isn't comfortable in the summer. But it wasn't because of the heat that I changed. It was because I didn't like going to see the Franciscans in my uniform. Unless I was on duty for some exceptional reason, I went every Saturday to go to confession and to make my financial donation.

I've been a Franciscan tertiary since 1934. The prosecutor never says a word about that. I don't say anything about it either because I think these days it could do the order some harm to have, or to have had, a tertiary like me. I'm almost sure Calvo Sotelo was a Franciscan tertiary, too, but I never came across him in any of our activities. If they ask me whether I'm a tertiary, I won't deny it, but if they don't I would rather not say anything about it. That's what I did before the war, too, because people are very confused about the subject and think being a tertiary is like being a monk, the only difference being that instead of wearing a habit you wear a uniform, in this case that of the Civil Guard. I'm not joking; that's what they think. And if you want to explain to them what being a tertiary involves, they cut you off: "No, it doesn't matter to me, whatever you want to be." As though they are humoring you.

But it's so simple you can explain it in three sentences. Tertiaries are as run-of-the-mill as any other men. The only difference is that, as much as we can, we join in the spirit of the order we belong to, which in the case of the Franciscans is the spirit of poverty. That's why I used to go on Saturdays. I gave whatever money I could, which in the end was a fair amount because after I had paid Emilia's dowry when she became a sister I didn't have many expenses other than José's tuition. I hardly had anything to spend money on.

On Saturdays, and also on Sundays, we distributed clothes to the poor. I would bring clothes contributed by my friends and colleagues who knew about this activity of mine. My general was one of them. He dressed very well, not just in his uniform but also in civilian clothes, and when he bought new clothes he would give me the old ones.

"Here, Escobar, for your poor."

"The poor belong to everybody, General."

"All right, so let's divide them up between us. How many do I get?"

We understood each other so well, Aranguren and I. Even during the war we would kid around with each other like that. I cried when I heard about the death he met, and writing this I have to look away to avoid blotting the page. I cry often, now, but only when I'm alone.

On the days I had to take old clothes I used my official car. An abuse. Sergeant Bermúdez, who had been my driver since 1933, would drive. He spent the entire war with me. My son Antonio says he's a bore because he never stops talking. But I like him.

Sergeant Bermúdez has always been a great organizer, and he would help the fathers distribute the clothes. First they would sort them, then clean them, sew them, and so forth, and when they were in proper shape distribute them to the people who needed them. People make fun of this handing out of used clothes—say it's just palming off hand-me-downs and calling it charity. That's because they haven't seen how useful the clothes are to the people who truly need them. To someone who ended up with a suit or overcoat of General Aranguren's, it was like winning the lottery.

That July 18 was a Saturday, and no sooner had I walked into the friary than the father in charge asked me, "Do you know anything about what they're saying has happened in Morocco?" I said no and then went to confession, to confess I had lied.

I'm a little offhand about confession. Sometimes I confess to things that aren't sins, just to fill out what I'm saying, and yet I'm sure I leave out some things that are. For example, my vanity and the pleasure I feel when I'm writing these notes, convinced that I'm the best writer in the Spanish army. I mean, I have the best penmanship. This would be a minor fault, and I don't think I should go to hell for it, but it's intriguing to feel the gratification that takes hold of me when I see how the pages pile up, covered with handwriting in which the finer strokes are differentiated from the bolder ones, all of the accents are where they should be, and the commas start off delicately, widen gradually, and end with a very subtle little tail. I've been meticulous about my handwriting since I was a child, but it turned into a passion when I became a sergeant. Every time a superior said to me, "Very good, Escobar, that's how a report should be written", I was so filled with self-satisfaction that I was afraid it showed all over my face. I hadn't turned twenty at that point, and my reaction was understandable because my father had instilled in me a sense of how many fine qualities I would need to have to be promoted. But now that I'm almost sixty, it's pure foolishness and vanity. My excuse now is that I need a distraction in this long period of solitary confinement.

Reports in the Spanish army—especially reports relating to personnel, which are the longest—have to be handwritten and composed very clearly. I had a teacher at the Civil Guard Academy in Getafe who would drill into us that the best way to develop that clarity was to read the classics. And that's what I did, in the academy's library. I would spend the whole afternoon there on Sundays. My father had died in Cuba by then, and Ramón and I didn't have an extra penny to spend on anything. Besides, the library had a huge fireplace, and in the winter it was the most comfortable room in the whole building. I read the books in alphabetical order, without skipping one, and when I finished with the Spaniards I went on to the Russians, to the French, and to the English. I don't remember the literature of any other nationality being represented in the library.

~

I left the Franciscans earlier than usual because I was worried. The friar in charge noticed it, and he looked at me suspiciously when I left. I told him, "I don't know much, Father, and the little I do know is an official secret. I hope you understand."

I said it with a smile, and he let me know he did understand. I was glad I said it, because he was one of the priests they killed a few days later.

I stopped at home to get back into uniform and could tell from the maid's face, without asking, that José hadn't returned. It was about eight in the evening. From that time on the tingling in my left arm didn't go away.

Brotons and my general were waiting for me in barracks. Brotons commanded the Rural Division of the Civil Guard. He was enthusiastic and naïve. He still thought, even near the end of the war, that the winners not only wouldn't punish us, they would respect rank. I was puzzled when the general told us the anarcho-syndicalists were armed. What's more, the story at the beginning was that the Generalitat had distributed the arms, but it became clear immediately that the anarchists had gotten them on their own.

Following instructions from the Generalitat's director of public order, Aranguren kept us in barracks for the night. He sometimes gave the impression of hoping that the Civil Guard could stay neutral in what very clearly was about to happen. But actually, it seemed incredible that it would in fact happen. The night couldn't have been more peaceful. It stayed calm, windless, a little hot, and people filled the terraces and cafés, drinking beer, *horchata*, and iced fruit crush, as though the next day were a holiday. So I mean that we public order professionals were sure something was bound to happen, but for people who weren't political activists—which would be more than 90 percent of the population—it was just another evening. The prosecutor doesn't see it that way. He maintains I should have foreseen everything that was going to happen, and therefore should have acted differently. The prosecutor is a young judge advocate captain who is doing his duty very zealously, which is natural because I'm the only commanding general of the Republican Army who is still alive and in Spain. The others are abroad. I wonder what will become of them. I think often of General Rojo. He, too, has suffered a lot.

Aranguren's dream of neutrality was impossible. The Civil Guard couldn't stand by with arms crossed while five thousand armed anarchists roamed the city streets. It pains me that people say or said that the Civil Guard was the traditional enemy of the anarchists. The Civil Guard's mission is to maintain order, and the anarchists didn't want that order. It was inevitable that we would have to take action against them. I'm not saying the order we had during the Republic was perfect, but I do believe it was worth doing everything we could to improve it. The prosecutor says that was my mistake: the order we had was unsustainable, and the military's obligation was to set another order—that is, the current order—in its place. They say it will now last forever. I hope that's true. But it seems impossible to me.

"Escobar," my general said to me that night, "how do you think we're going to be able to keep the lid on five thousand anarchists and at the same time put down our comrades who've rebelled?"

I think he said it that way, and the one who answered for me was Brotons, who thought the Civil Guard was the best-prepared corps of the whole Spanish army and therefore up to the challenge we had coming at us. His enthusiasm almost made us laugh.

I argued to my general that, according to the information we had, the only regiments that would revolt were the Badajoz Infantry, the Artillery, and the Cavalry. General Llano de la Encomienda, the commander of the division, was confident of the loyalty of the rest of the garrison, as well as of the air forces at Prat. So it was reasonable to think the uprising would be suppressed by the soldiers themselves, and that we would be called upon to do no more than the usual: restore public order.

I remember General Aranguren asking me, "And in the rest of Spain, what'll happen there?"

"I don't know, General."

That was certainly true as far as it went. But if I had told the whole truth, I might have given this outrageous answer: I don't know, General, and I don't care. How myopic we are. What preyed on my mind that night was what would happen to my son José, who was so damaged and who had lost his mother when he was barely sixteen, the worst possible age. But I was worried about what might happen that night and the next day, and I thought if I managed to keep him out of the fighting for a few hours, I would be able to find a long-term solution later.

Colonel Brotons took me aside and said, "Listen, Antonio, the rebels are using civilians. Do you know anything about your son?"

He said it because he knew José was a member of the Falange. I think I gave him a little bit of a cold shoulder and didn't react to his overture.

I didn't know anything about my boy. I had Sergeant Bermúdez out looking for him all night, anywhere in the city he might be, without success. Every time he came back from one of these forays, the sergeant would say to me, "Don't worry, Colonel, I'll keep my eyes peeled."

More foolish this advice couldn't have been, but it helped me. Enough so that a little before dawn the pins and needles in my arm went away, and I slept for a while.

~

Before he was a bullfighter, my brother Alberto was a football player and played on a team in Valencia, in a youth league, that reached the finals of the Spanish championships that year. After the game—which his team won, I think—I asked him, "How was the game, Alberto?"

"You'd know better than I would. You saw it; I was in it."

His answer became a family joke. When somebody got

lost in the high weeds we would say, "So-and-so didn't understand anything because he was in it."

I was in it, that July 19, and all I could understand was what was going on around me. The prosecutor, though, must have had a seat particularly high up in the stands because he knows what happened both on and off the field. He can't understand how I could have failed to see that Spain was permanently divided into two teams, and that I should have been playing on the other one.

I don't know why I use this analogy. I barely understand football, and I haven't seen a game since Alberto stopped playing.

I remember that I couldn't have been all that deaf that morning, because the ringing of the bells for the first Mass of the day woke me up. Barcelona is so beautiful early on a summer Sunday. The streets were almost empty. There were women riding their bicycles to church, the baker, a family getting ready to spend the day at the beach, not much more.

I suppose I didn't hear it, but I *felt* the tramp of infantry soldiers on the march. I enlisted as a volunteer in 1895, when I was sixteen years and one day old, so although it doesn't reach me through my ears, I feel the vibrations that bring me the rhythm of troops marching in step. When I'm walking alone in the street, I keep step. Maybe I don't know how to walk any other way. My lawyer wants to base my defense on that: that I've been so thoroughly molded as a Civil Guard that I was acting under influences that limited my freedom of choice. That's not Christian. I'm not saying that what my lawyer is trying to do isn't Christian, because he's a man of honor and in better hands I could not be. But what isn't Christian is the idea that my freedom as a man, and all that that implies, could be limited by superficial factors like that one. I remember that whenever he saw me, General Miaja would greet me with, "Here comes the Civilest Guard!" He would say it to me even after I became a general of the Republican Army. I didn't think it was funny at all, even though he meant it positively, almost as praise. But if you think a Civil Guard is a man you put into a uniform and wind up to set him to work, you don't know us.

What I did hear was the metallic grinding of the artillery regiment's gun carriages. The sound carried all the way out to the Ronda de San Pedro. The fighting began a little later.

It was a trivial thing, but I was struck by the flocks of pigeons in the Plaza de Cataluña that took off at the first shots, spread out over the neighborhoods nearby, and flocked together to head back to the plaza, but then, because the shooting never stopped, scattered again.

Brotons was with his Rural Division, I don't know where, and General Aranguren was at the Generalitat. I was at my command post, of course, with the Nineteenth Division, the Urban Division, in our barracks on the Calle Ausiàs March.

I called home, without telling Sergeant Bermúdez because I didn't want him to take it as a sign that I didn't have confidence in his motivation or effectiveness, and the maid confirmed what I already knew: José hadn't slept there. The pain around my heart was so sharp that the pins and needles radiated not only through my left arm but down through my left leg to the tips of my toes. It came to me that if this was a symptom of a heart attack, as people say, it would all be over in a second. I tried to calm myself down to prevent that, because I would bring disgrace on the Corps by dying that way at such a moment.

A captain came to my office in the middle of the morning and told me, "Colonel, Generals Burriel and Legórburu have taken over the Telefónica building and the Hotel Colón."

He didn't try to hide his satisfaction, taking for granted that I knew those two generals were at the head of the uprising. The captain was young, a graduate of the academy in Toledo like my brother Alfredo and my son Antonio.

"Thank you. Return to your post."

It wasn't part of his assignment to report that information, so I put him under watch and in the end had to arrest him.

It was a very tense morning. All the Guards were in barracks, listening to the gunfire and explosions that made it clear there was a genuine head-to-head battle going on. The booming of the artillery particularly impressed us, because the Civil Guard isn't familiar with weapons of that kind. A cannon is a weapon of war, and the Civil Guard is there to keep the peace. My father, who suffered through so many wars, from the Carlists to Cuba, where he lost his life, was the one who set us on a course of study that would qualify us to join the Corps. He thought it was a great advantage to be able to serve without having to leave the peninsula or nearby islands. As I remember, he made two trips to Cuba. My mother suffered over them a great deal, but he never became discouraged. He would say, "I can't complain. There's a difference between going to Cuba as a major and going as an immigrant, or a stowaway, to work on the docks in Havana."

It's relevant that my father was born in the province of Lugo, in Alvaredo, which is a miserable little hamlet, or was. The people there who emigrated to America—that is, most of the inhabitants—worked there in very menial jobs, and not that many of them came back having made their fortune. My father met quite a few civilians in Cuba who were surprised by his military career. A major in His Majesty's army was somebody to be admired. I admired him, too. My father enlisted as a volunteer at the age of twenty-one, and all his promotions after he made corporal were for his service in war. That's why he rejected it for his sons and wanted us to go into the Civil Guard, so we wouldn't have to serve in a war. Obviously, man proposes and God disposes. Of his three sons who joined the Civil Guard, the two of us who are still in active service have had to serve in a war, and on opposite sides. Yet Alfredo and I love each other. For the Escobar family, it's not just a manner of speaking to say this war is fratricidal. And the same thing has happened to my sons.

~

When I went back to Barcelona in January 1937, President Azaña invited me to dinner at Pedralbes and introduced me to the other guests this way: "Colonel Escobar, whose action at the head of the Civil Guard on July 19 tipped the fight in Barcelona in favor of the legally constituted order of things."

I know he has repeated this several times and has even written it.

"But don't worry," he told me another time, "nobody's going to thank you for it." Everything the president says has a touch of bitterness about it.

Of course the prosecutor not only does not thank me for it, but maintains that, because of men like me, what should have been just a simple reestablishment of order became a civil war. My admirer Azaña said that if there had been a dozen anticoup soldiers like me the war wouldn't have happened.

Life is very complicated, and only God knows.

That morning, around noon, General Goded arrived from Palma de Mallorca in a seaplane. He had been named to head the uprising in Catalonia. I didn't know him well but remembered him as a zealous monarchist soldier. We didn't think the other general we supposed was at the head of the revolt in Spain—I'm talking about Mola—was a dyed-in-the-wool monarchist. He had even served the Republic. But he must have turned into a monarchist by now, although not in support of the same dynastic line as Goded's faction, because Mola began the war in the north of Spain at the head of Carlist troops. That seemed like an anachronism to me, because I remembered that my father was awarded the medal for Meritorious Service as an Illustrious Son of the Fatherland for his role in putting down the Carlist insurrection. But that was in the last century.

General Goded was able to get to the captaincy general and telephoned my general from there to demand intervention by the Civil Guard in his support. It passes all understanding how he could have thought he had the least authority to require something like that of General Aranguren. Since in fact Goded didn't have it, he threatened Aranguren with being shot when the uprising triumphed. My general answered him, "If you shoot me tomorrow, you'll have shot a general who's kept his word and fulfilled his sworn duty as a soldier."

I enjoy writing this down. In such a lonely time I sometimes feel disoriented, and it makes me feel better to record what my superiors and friends said and thought.

A little later, my general called me and gave me instructions. I don't remember them very precisely, and I'm not interested in remembering them. My lawyer pushes me hard to say that I was just following the strict orders of my superior in the chain of command, General Aranguren, because due obedience is a legal defense. The truth is, though, that the way things stand, I would rather be judged by God. I'll fare better.

And I can't say it because my general didn't give me strict orders.

Some charitable soul has gotten word to me that General Aranguren, trying to save his life in his court-martial in Valencia, testified that he took the position he did because of the pressure Brotons and I brought to bear on him. I don't believe it.

If I say that my general limited himself to telling me to do whatever was required under the circumstances, I don't think I'm straying too far from the truth.

We left the barracks at four in the afternoon. I marched at the head of two columns of five hundred men each, with each man armed as the regulations require.

When we reached Vía Layetana I gave the order to

mark time. I did it because, on that disordered day, I didn't want us to be seen as being among the men who were joining in the chaos. From that moment on I had a sensation of silence, and not because my deafness was getting worse. The silence descended as we marched along. People whom we normally would have had to put in jail fell back out of our way to let us go by. I'm talking about civilians with flails, cartridge belts, rifles, and pistols. My Guards looked at them sidelong and, I suppose, thought the same way I did. One of my junior officers did catch my eye, as though he was awaiting instructions, but I kept on marching. Because the crowd was receding as we passed, I conceived the illusion that, when the legitimate representatives of law and order showed up, the civilians would yield the role they had assumed in the emergency created by the insurrection.

On our way, which could lead to only one destination, we had to pass by the headquarters of the Commission of Public Order at the Generalitat. I've mentioned that I use my eyesight to compensate for what I lack in hearing, and it served me that day in my noticing how Escofet, who was the general commissioner of public order, having been advised that we were coming, went out onto the balcony and then called for the president to join him. Companys thought it was a good moment for that, and he came out trying to strike a pose that would inspire confidence. I remember he stood erect and put both hands on the railing, but he then instantly pulled them back because the railing was made of iron and was burning hot in the strong July sun. This unsettled him, but he was still the president of the entity we served, so I myself called out the order to halt. When your troops are a large group, as they were in this case, you have to take care to give the order in two parts: the cautionary command, which is drawn out to give prior notice, and the executive command, which is cut short and sharp so the sound of heels meeting pavement will also be short and sharp. Shut up here in my cell, I feel nostalgic when I look back on these details of my service. I also paid a lot of attention to close-order drill. When it's well done, the individuals in the unit form a bond in close-order drill that serves them well in much more than the simple mechanics of the drill maneuvers. So it seems to me. I suffered a lot at the beginning of the war when the people's militias, under the pretext that drill was just a ploy to limit revolutionary action, moved so chaotically that it made you blush. But not a puritanical blush: a sad and painful one, because those poor, unlucky men would drop like flies facing the trained troops of the Army of Africa in battle. Especially in the battle for Madrid in November 1936. It was horrible. The Communists were the first ones to admit that it was impossible to go on fighting as a disorganized mob, and that we had to be in formation. That was why Prime Minister Negrín leaned so heavily on them for support. They seemed to him to be a lesser evil—the possibility of order in the midst of chaos. I never went along with Communism, and they can't accuse me of that in my trial. In March of 1939 I put down the Communist movement when I was the commanding general of the Army of Extremadura.

I didn't turn toward President Companys until I could *feel* that the voice in which I'd given my commands had had the desired effect and the two columns were solidly set in the right stance. I thought it was vital to project a feeling of correctness and normalcy, as the only answer in a situation where resorting to force as a solution would cause so many collateral problems. And to convey that sense of normalcy I said to President Companys what I always said when I was with him: "At your service, Mr. President."

A set phrase from the regulations, but on this occasion it wasn't, or it was understood as being more than that. Escofet, Guarner, and Tarradellas, as I remember, were on the balcony along with Companys. One of them—Escofet, I think—called for *vivas* for the Civil Guard, and the audience in the street replied in unison. I suppose that would be the same audience that at other times called us murderers at the top of their lungs. Some of the women came up to the troops to show their appreciation for them, but the Guards stood rock-solid, like statues, and the sergeants turned the people away. It affects me to remember those Guards, most of them fathers of families. So many of them, surely, have died.

We resumed our march toward the Plaza de Cataluña to make our approach to the Hotel Colón. Sergeant Bermúdez, who wasn't in the formation, warned me, "The Hotel Colón is where there are civilian elements who are supporting the soldiers."

I deployed the Guards but ordered them not to open fire.

When I saw the bodies in the Plaza de Cataluña my

spirits sank, not for myself but because I understood that the spilling of so much blood couldn't be resolved with mere disciplinary measures.

At that point, I didn't know whether I wanted to save Spain or my son José.

These are scruples of conscience that I have to put behind me, because the one wasn't incompatible with the other.

I remember that a militiaman sitting behind a machine gun tripod aimed it at me, but an Assault Guard took it over, swiftly cutting off the move.

What I heard above all, I remember, was silence. Some armed groups shot at the hotel, as a gesture in support of my advance, and I asked for a cease-fire. They say that Durruti endorsed my order. I don't know. What I do know is what I did. And when I headed for the Hotel Colón it of course didn't occur to me even for a second to take out my pistol. I haven't read it, but I've been told that a French writer who was a pilot in the war on our side has published a book in which he describes me, under a pseudonym, as fighting heroically against the rebels with a pistol in my hand. I thank him for that, but that's not how it was.

I didn't take it out because I had my swagger stick, and if that wasn't adequate for what I had to do, an automatic with nine bullets would have been much less so.

I approached the front door of the hotel while my Guards took their places in a semicircle. I don't suppose the prosecutor will believe it, but I ordered them to assume this position to prevent the people's militias from entering the hotel and retaliating for the many corpses that were scattered around the Plaza. The idea that the militias could have protected me was a fiction, if you consider that they were armed with Mausers and carbines, up against the rebels' machine guns and artillery.

I went in through a revolving door with four compartments, like the ones you see in cartoons where the person in it begins to go around and around and can't get out. Well, something like that happened. Not to me but to the Guards that followed me, who entered by twos and got wedged in. It was a disconcerting bit of absurdity. A rebel lieutenant colonel stood facing me with a pistol in his hand, looking forward to seeing how their entry would unfold. I think, and people have told me, that from the outside my demeanor seemed very self-possessed, just involuntarily. But to me, inside the hotel, it was unsettling because rather than addressing myself to the lieutenant colonel I had to set about freeing my Guards. They began to come in very smoothly once they got the hang of the contraption. So before I had said a word there were more than fifty of them standing in the lobby.

"You have to lay down your arms" was the first thing I said. "You'll be evacuated under our orders."

"Under what authority are you acting?" the lieutenant colonel asked me.

"The authority of the Generalitat."

"And General Goded?"

"I don't know anything about him."

I wasn't lying because I didn't even know at that point about the conversation that Goded had had with my general. The lieutenant colonel may have interpreted my ignorance differently. As though if I had known what General Goded was doing I would have fallen in behind him. I realized that the situation was now under control, because once the problem of that blessed revolving door had been solved my Guards came in without a hitch and were spreading out around the whole lobby.

God seemed to have heard my prayers because up on the mezzanine, near a window padded with cushions, José was standing in his Falangist blue shirt with a rifle in his hand. There were other civilians, but wearing ties, who when they saw what was happening dropped their rifles and hid in the corridors. I suppose they went to mix in with the hotel guests who were in their rooms. But we Escobars have always been very attached to uniforms, and there was José showing off his so there would be no doubt that he was a rebel rising up in arms. He looked younger and thinner than ever.

I expressly ordered the captain in command of the company not to let anybody into the hotel besides the forces of public order, and to get ready to evacuate the rebels.

I think I correctly followed my general's order to do what needed to be done under the circumstances. Outside, no action was taken against the anarchists who, at least while I was advancing among them, accepted the order I represented. As for the inside of the hotel, I limited myself to asking the rebels to lay down their arms. I didn't even demand their surrender, because that wasn't part of my job.

As far as the other question is concerned, I'll never know whether I was up to the mark of what needed to be done under the circumstances. I'm talking about when

I instructed Sergeant Bermúdez, "Now go about your business."

"Yes, Colonel."

Sergeant Bermúdez was authorized not only to take José's rifle away from him but also to give him a couple of whacks because he had known him, I reckoned, since he was twelve. He taught him how to poach in Villalba, when my son Antonio was there as a lieutenant of the Civil Guard.

~

They set me up in the hotel manager's office, to direct the removal. I called my general and updated him. He approved what I had done and thanked me. He thanked me with sadness in his voice. I wasn't so sad because, naïvely, I thought José was safe, to the point that the pain in and around my heart had completely disappeared. Also, I was pretty satisfied with the performance of the Civil Guard. I thought if that performance was being duplicated in other major cities, yet another random military coup had been snuffed out. Since at that point I didn't know the scale of what was involved, and the only evident action in peninsular Spain was Mola's uprising at the head of the Carlists, I got the feeling that fighting the Carlists had become a recurring occupation of our family. I think I've already explained that my father had been recognized for his "meritorious service as an illustrious son of the Fatherland", for his contribution to putting down the last Carlist insurrection. My brother Ramón and I, who are the eldest brothers, took pride in that distinction, but our younger brothers, Alfredo and Alberto, made a joke out of their being the sons of someone who was an "illustrious son of the Fatherland".

That rebellion was in 1876, and it seemed odd to me that General Mola should have resumed it—sixty years later.

President Companys called me at the hotel to congratulate me, and that was when I got my first cold shower.

His congratulations were more than polite, and they were mixed with a touch of penitence. He had always mistrusted me because of what he called my "Catholic militancy". Intelligent and well-informed though he was, he thought those of us who went to Mass every day got our instructions from the Vatican. That might not be a fair thing for me to say, especially about a man who, from what I've heard, is at this point in a situation not very different from mine. Besides, we took risks together that enabled us to save many lives. My counsel stresses this point, but the prosecutor insists that for every life I saved, I contributed to the loss of many more.

I could testify in Companys' favor in his trial, wherever and whenever it might be held. But my testimony, and what I could swear to, wouldn't be worth much. That's strange, because I've fought shoulder-to-shoulder with him on a side with which I had so little affinity, in order to fulfill my oath. But the other side thinks my oath is worthless. Fortunately, the one who will definitively decide what it's worth is God: it was in his name that I took it.

After thanking the president for his congratulations I explained to him my plan for evacuating the hotel, which he approved. But it was when I asked him for instructions on disarming the syndicalists that I got that first cold shower.

"We're going to have to negotiate with them, Escobar. At this point the city belongs to them."

It's not true that the Civil Guard obeys orders blindly. At least, I always made sure I explained them and got others to explain them to me, and what President Companys was saying was inexplicable. So I reminded him that our forces at the airfield were under the control of Colonel Díaz Sandino, and that the head of the division himself, General Llano de la Encomienda, was still following the orders of the government.

"I'm telling you, Colonel, that it's our job to negotiate."

He was referring to the politicians. What's more, I had noticed that when he addressed me by rank it was to put me in my place. And this time around it was hard for me to accept because with all the security forces he had, and with the army at the disposal of the government, I didn't understand his giving in like that.

I understood it even less because the armed syndicalists kept a safe distance from my Civil Guard, so we would have no problem evacuating the hotel through the service entrance, which is where our wagons were waiting.

I can't let this point go. I make a lot of mistakes every day as a man, but fewer as a Civil Guard, because being a Civil Guard is easier than being a man. When the Urban Division I was commanding stepped in as I've described, the syndicalists' activity was important as a harassment of the rebel troops, who weren't able to relax.

But there weren't that many of the syndicalists, and they were lightly armed. It was only after our move on the Hotel Colón and the rebels' surrender that the number of available weapons increased, as did the number of civilians—men and women—who were ready to grab them. And so there came a time when the syndicalists, with army weapons, could exercise their authority over the city.

Up until that point, when the number of armed anarchists was still small, we could and should have cut off what later degenerated into a revolution within the legally constituted regime. During my march up Vía Layetana at the head of my men, I thought I had two jobs to do: one, to put down an insurrection that didn't seem to be very well prepared, at least as far as Barcelona was concerned; and the other, to disarm the anarchists. The first job wasn't hard. The second took months and cost a lot of blood, including a few liters of mine. I turned out to seem like something of a contradiction in this war, because I fought the whole time not just against the rebellion but also against the internal revolution. And, so I've heard, because I never failed to use the correct forms of military address or to accomplish my military mission . . . or even to unbutton the collar of my Corps jacket.

~

My annoyance tailed off, or I forgot about it, as soon as Sergeant Bermúdez's face appeared at the door of my makeshift office. He was wearing his usual "Everything's in order, Colonel" expression. Bermúdez is obsessed with not having me worry about anything: everything's always in order. If we had a flat tire—which at the end of the war happened often—he would say to me: "We have a flat tire, General, but don't worry." It was his motto, and it never changed. So when he told me in 1936, in the retreat from the battle of Navalcarnero, "A mortar's going to land on us, Colonel, but don't worry," I thought it was a joke. Well, no: the mortar did land. But Sergeant Bermúdez gave the steering wheel of the Ford T we were in such a wrench that the only effect we felt was from the expansion wave, which blew us into a fallow field. We ended up with a few bruises.

This time I understood the meaning of the expression on his face, and I asked the captain adjutant who was in the office to leave us to ourselves. I did it to spare him embarrassment, not to hide anything from him, because the whole division knew about my son the Falangist, who was now there in front of me, still in his blue shirt. At least he wasn't carrying his rifle. Sergeant Bermúdez brought him into the office and went out again, so we could be alone.

The first thing I did was to tell him off. "What's this all about? You wanted to save Spain, is that it?"

Looking scared, the boy stared at the floor.

"And if possible, all by yourself, right?"

José had a very handsome face, like his mother's, and because he didn't have the typical Escobar beefiness he gave the impression of being fragile. I think it was misleading because, although his body was very lean, it was also very muscular.

"Thanks to you, I haven't been able to sleep all night!

Hours go by with no sign of life from you, while I'm trying to figure out where you could be. Unfortunately, I wasn't wrong!"

"I'm sorry, Father."

He said it so remorsefully and so politely and respectfully, which is how he always was with me, that I had to yell some more to avoid bursting into tears right then and there.

"But don't you realize this uprising's crazy? That if we don't stop it right away it could end up turning into a civil war? And wars never solve anything!"

Fortunately he said the most unwelcome thing I could have heard. "I understand, Father, that given the uniform you wear you have to think that way, but—"

I didn't let him go on because this time, when I yelled at him, I didn't need to pretend I was angry: "Leave my uniform out of it! I don't think with my uniform, I think with my head!"

He fell silent immediately, head down. I think it was the first time in my life I ever had a fight with him. And the last, of course. When I became a widower I had already lost two children—to sudden, unknown illnesses—and it seemed to me that this youngest son was my reason for living on. Antonio, when he graduated as a lieutenant from the academy in Toledo, requested a posting in Africa. He joined the Corps when he came back, and then he married Angelita right away. And Emilia took her vows as a sister, as I've said. So just the two of us, José and I, were left by ourselves. Maybe where I went wrong was in not paying more attention to politics. I paid so little, in fact, that the first time I saw José dressed in his blue shirt I thought it was a Boy Scout uniform of some kind or other.

"And take off that shirt! You're not allowed to wear the uniform of an illegal party! Sergeant!"

Sergeant Bermúdez appeared immediately, having been standing outside pressed up against the door. I didn't need to shout at the boy as much as I did, because he wasn't about to argue with my orders at such a delicate moment. It was delicate because, as I was talking to him, I was watching the evacuation of the hotel through the window and realized that people were shouting at the soldiers more and more, as they were going out through a double file of my Civil Guards. The Assault Guards also performed very well and established a cordon to keep the syndicalists at bay. That's why I say that, at that point, they still respected us and we could have handled the situation. All we needed was for General Llano de la Encomienda to deploy loyal troops on the street to support us. I don't understand why he didn't.

I sent Sergeant Bermúdez to get some civilian clothes for José. He disappeared without asking where he should look for them. Bermúdez may be a bore when he's talking, but when he knows he must, he keeps quiet and asks no questions.

Since we were alone again, José dared to ask shyly, "Father, what are you going to do?"

"What I should have done when I found out you were getting involved in this mess. You're going to take the first ship to Italy, even if it's a freighter! From now on your aunt and sister will look after you there."

Fortunately, the prosecutor doesn't know yet that I have

a sister, Dolores, who is a nun. If he finds out, he'll consider me a traitor not only to my country and my God, but also to my family. She's a social worker, along with my daughter, and at this point both of them were in a convent in Italy. That's why I thought of sending José there. When he heard that, he struck a very charming pose of high-mindedness: "Father, I don't want to use you as an excuse for shirking my responsibilities."

Truly: I didn't know whether to laugh or cry at this point. I took him by the arm and led him to the window so he could watch the evacuation of the soldiers. "Look," I said, "many of those men will be tried, and I'm sure most of them will be let go because following orders isn't a crime. But, a civilian who belongs to an underground party, who wears a uniform that he's not allowed to wear, who's seized with a rifle in his hand—he's engaged in an uprising against the legally constituted government! A man like that would be shot. You understand? *Shot*!"

I didn't get the feeling that my words impressed him all that much, and if he maintained his remorseful expression, I think it was because he had never seen me angry in his life. I felt such tenderness that I almost begged him, "What is it? Aren't you afraid to die?"

He said to me, with a very appealing expression, "But when you went into the hotel alone, Father, you didn't seem to be afraid to die either."

What a child, making a plaything of his life, which was the most important thing in mine. I had to make an effort to work myself back up into being angry. "Die? Dying's part of my job! That's what they pay me for!"

I learned that from my father. He always had a great sense of his job as a profession. He would say to us, "This is a good job and very well paid"—I repeat, his fellow villagers in Alvaredo were working in the most miserable jobs, whether at home or in the Americas—"but you have to give value for your money, even with your life." He gave every penny's worth of his pay, and it seems to me that, since the prosecutor is going to have his way, I'm not going to be far behind him. My father died a hero, there's no doubt about that.

Sergeant Bermúdez poked his head in the door as I was finishing my harangue, but he closed it again when he saw the mood I was in. There was no time to waste, so I stopped talking, and as soon as silence fell the sergeant came in with civilian clothes. Without looking at me, he said to the boy, "Here, this'll do for you."

He said it with great assurance and annoyance. Sergeant Bermúdez is a confirmed bachelor, and José meant a lot to him, too. The sergeant was the one who taught him how to drive, and he let him drive the official car on the sly.

I ordered him to bring a car, with some Civil Guards he trusted, and park it in a place where it wouldn't attract attention.

José, very obedient now, began to change his clothes, and when I saw his sunken chest I made a silly comment: "José, you have to take better care of yourself, especially in what you eat. Look at how solid your brother Antonio is." This is what his mother always said to him.

"Yes, Father," he said.

"You're going straight to the harbor now, but you have to promise me you'll stay in Italy until all this is over."

"I wouldn't want to make a promise that I don't know I'm going to keep."

I had to repeat this statement to myself because at first, between my deafness and being distracted by the noises coming up from the street, I didn't hear it very clearly. To the point where I said, "So we're in agreement, right?"

"No, Father."

"What do you mean, no?" I said in surprise.

He changed his expression abruptly and adopted the bold one he used to put on when he was bluffing in one of our card games.

"Yes, Father, I think we're in agreement that I shouldn't make you a promise that anyway I can't keep."

"Why won't you be able to keep it?"

I said it to him in such an imploring tone that I realized I was past hope.

"You said yourself that there could be a war. And I couldn't leave my friends—"

I gave it one more try, hardening my voice. "If your friends go home and the people down there shouting in the street do the same, there won't be a war! This is a problem for professionals! Let us handle it!"

Given the circumstances I didn't want to say good-bye to my son in a shouting match, so I out-and-out begged him, "When I went into the hotel unarmed this afternoon, and I ordered my men not to shoot, I was sure you were there, . . . and I was afraid you'd be wounded."

I don't know, maybe I was lying to lean on him, but my eyes filled with tears. What I do know is that what I said next was true: "I've lost two children and your mother. God be praised, but I couldn't stand losing you, too."

I'll never forget José's face at that moment, and I seized the chance to beg him: "Can't you make me the promise I'm asking for?"

The boy stood still as a statue, dropping the expression of bravado he had assumed earlier, and if he did make a gesture with his head it was clearly negative. Neither of us could take any more, so I took advantage of the fact that Sergeant Bermúdez had done what he always does, appearing and disappearing at the door so we would know he was waiting. "All right, son," I said, "the car's here. The sooner you go the better."

I said that *son* very affectionately so he wouldn't think I was still angry. He was the one who threw himself into my arms, and to comfort him I cracked a joke: "Relax. I'll try to end this war before you have time to come back."

Who would have thought it would last so long? For me, it's still going on. I don't know when it will end.

~

That same afternoon I was summoned to attend General Goded's surrender. It took place in the headquarters of the captaincy general, and the people present, as I remember, were President Companys; the commander of the division, General Llano de la Encomienda; General Aranguren; and other lower-ranking commanders. There were also some civilians, one of whom was Durruti. I knew him well.

General Goded agreed to speak on the radio, as Companys explained beforehand, to avoid pointless bloodshed.

Goded said his luck had turned against him, he considered himself a prisoner, and therefore he was releasing his comrades from the commitment they had made to him.

I suppose he realized he was signing his death sentence, but his voice didn't waver even for a moment. His sentence might have been commuted if the uprising had been put down, but it wasn't, and they executed him here in this same castle of Montjuich where I'm being held. I'm occupying his cell because it's the one that's assigned to the highest-ranking officer, which he was then and I am now.

Because the castle is near the harbor the sea breeze reaches me here, and I also occasionally see the seagulls flying by. I've been in this cell for eight months—Goded's stay was shorter—and waking up in the summer was a pleasure thanks to the chirping of the birds, which Barcelona has always had many of. But we are getting into winter, so the dawns come late and foggy, and all I can hear now is the screeching of the gulls.

When General Goded finished his short radio speech, two captains took him away. We soldiers who witnessed the moment all had a knot in our throats. President Companys, on the other hand, was very pleased because the broadcast was relayed throughout Spain and he thought this message of surrender would have a very positive effect.

General Aranguren took me by the arm and led me onto the balcony that looked out over the Paseo de Colón. My general was more affected than I was, and he repeated to me, "It's going to be so hard to fight against our comrades!"

I felt that less keenly than he did because at least I could console myself with having taken my youngest child out of the conflict. I knew he was in the hands of Sergeant Bermúdez, who would either see him onto a ship bound for Italy or die trying. So, despite the seriousness of the situation and the pain of witnessing the surrender of an honorable soldier who was thereby setting himself on a path to the scaffold, I felt a slight touch of relief. May God forgive me for my selfishness, although I don't suppose he will have to forgive me for being a father.

"None of our comrades has the right to rise up against the legitimately constituted government and take us to the edge of civil war. It's our obligation to prevent it," I argued.

"I admire your conviction, Escobar. I wish I had it."

I suppose my conviction was theoretical or, rather, reasoned, but confusion was eating away at me inside. He made a telling thrust when he said, "But do you realize, Escobar, that we're fighting alongside the anarchists?"

"Let's hope we won't be for long, General."

But this venting wasn't the main point. The reason he had taken me onto the balcony was to talk to me about a group of rebel officers who were holed up in the monastery on Calle Lauria. Apparently they were still fighting.

I argued that they would turn over their weapons as soon as they heard about General Goded's message of surrender. My general nodded in agreement, but he added his real worry: "Yes, but the problem is that the people outside in the street think the Carmelite friars have fortified themselves in the church."

"Who controls the perimeter of the monastery?"

"Two companies of Assault Guards."

The general saw I wasn't eager to intervene, especially given that other security forces were involved and they were perfectly competent. So he went on, "There are also ordinary people harassing, and some groups of anarchists."

The way I saw it, the concentrations of rebel resistance should be rooted out by General Llano de la Encomienda's troops, after which it would be the Civil Guard's job to restore public order.

The general said something very funny to me: "As a matter of fact, Escobar, aren't you a tertiary of the Carmelites, as it happens?"

"No, General, I'm a tertiary of the Franciscans."

I had explained this to him a dozen times and he always nodded politely at what I said, but he didn't understand much of it. Even so, he was a good Catholic. It was clear, though, that his ingenuous question was aimed at pressuring me.

"What's this about, General, do you want me to go to the monastery?"

"I'd feel better if you did, Escobar."

~

I took the Civil Guards to Calle Lauria in four wagons. People cheered us along the way, and my troops started to respond to the cheers, but I quickly cut them off. One of my Guards raised his fist, and I ordered his arrest. When he's in uniform, a Guard shouldn't make any moves that aren't prescribed in the regulations. It's not that I love regulations; it's common sense. Our authority at that point was rooted in people's perception that we were doing our duty independently of our inner feelings.

A captain of the Assault Guards, who didn't hide his satisfaction over our arrival, was waiting for me near the monastery. He was an appealing young man.

"I'm glad you've come, Colonel," he said to me.

He had his men well positioned, and the silence inside the monastery was complete. So I asked him, "Why didn't you try to bring them out?"

"I was worried about the militias. They're convinced the monks have armed themselves."

"What's that about? They can't tell a uniform from a cassock?"

The kid laughed. Judging from the fact that he was already a captain, he must have graduated from the academy in Toledo, so I asked him if he knew my son Antonio.

"Yes, Colonel, we were buddies there, and then we were together in Africa. He told us about you and his grandfather, your father."

"Who, the illustrious son of the Fatherland?"

This was no time to talk family, but as I took over in a situation whose seriousness I didn't underestimate for a minute, I was just trying to give the Assault Guards captain confidence because I could see he was rattled. People were moving in our direction through the streets nearby, looking at the monastery and then at us. Some of them were retrieving wounded militiamen. I also saw them recover a body. The monastery had ogival windows, with rifles sticking out of them. What sadness.

"How long has it been since the last shot was fired?" I asked the Assault Guards captain.

"I'd say fifteen minutes."

"And why aren't the militia after them, either?"

"We succeeded in separating them."

"That's good."

All the same, I realized that the anarcho-syndicalists were regrouping in the nighttime darkness behind us and piling sandbags on a knoll to our left, where they were going to set up a machine gun tripod. So I said to the captain, "All right, Captain. The sooner we get this done the better."

It seems as though I've made that line my personal motto.

I deployed my Guards in front of the main façade, with some along each side. Since I had less confidence in the Assault Guards, I ordered their captain to hold them in their reserve position and to keep an eye on the syndicalists.

I stepped out and moved alone toward the front door of the monastery. My officers know they have to wait a little while before they advance to cover me. My experience is that it's harder to shoot at a lone man. In spite of everything, I was sweating from the tension of the moment, the heat of the airless night, the tightness of my uniform, and twenty-four almost sleepless hours; and maybe out of fear, too. I remember that as I moved forward I tried to get what little protection I could from the trees that are, or were, in the street. I saw some of the rifles disappear from the ogival windows, and that gave me confidence.

When I reached the door I rapped it with the butt of

my swagger stick. Obviously, I didn't pull out my pistol this time, either. A colonel of the Civil Guard should use his weapon only very rarely. The door had a slit in it, as monastery doors do, and a soldier was peering out. He was wearing a barracks cap with three eight-pointed stars. I saluted him formally and said, "Colonel, you have to hand yourselves over."

"On what conditions?" he asked.

"Did you hear General Goded's statement on the radio?"

"Yes, sir."

"So you know this is all about avoiding pointless bloodshed."

I couldn't say anything else, and he couldn't expect me to, because my Guards had taken up well-chosen positions, including up against the façade outside the defenders' field of fire. I thought I was doing the rebels a favor by offering them the chance to surrender.

"How will we get out of here?" he asked me, and I realized that that was his real worry, which was reasonable because the threatening sounds of the crowd at my back were coming through to us.

"In our wagons; the sooner the better. Leave your weapons inside. Where are the monks?"

"In the crypt," he answered.

"So tell them not to move."

"Wait a moment. I'm going to consult my comrades."

"No, don't consult your comrades!" I insisted. "Trust me."

I think he did both things, more or less. He wasted almost a quarter of an hour doing the first one, and that was too long under the circumstances. We had managed to place our wagons close to the door, where it was easy to form a double file of Guards as a kind of corridor. The evacuation began well even with the delay, although as the soldiers came out the shouts and insults from the crowd increased. But we Civil Guards are used to working under conditions like these.

At a guess, at least thirty soldiers or so boarded the first wagon, and they weren't hurt.

The first shots began when monks started to come out of a side door that we didn't have as firmly under our control. I couldn't believe it, and I thought the poor monks had lost their minds. My idea had been to remove the soldiers and leave a detachment of my Guards to protect the monastery and the monks. At that point we didn't know the dimensions of the coming revolution, or its anticlerical nature.

The prosecutor says only a fool like me would have been so unaware. He doesn't say it in those words, but the implication is clear.

This tragic, reckless surfacing of the monks was caused by a fire set by the anarchists in the monastery basement. They went up to the building from behind, where there was a solid wall that we had therefore left practically unprotected, but it had air vents at ground level, through which they threw bottles of gasoline with flaming wicks. The fire spread quickly because the building was old and had a wood frame. Before we knew it on the outside the monks, having holed up in the basement crypt, were suffocating from the smoke. They had no choice but to come out. I emphatically believe that the fifteen minutes the colonel spent making up his mind did us a lot of damage, because that gave the militias time to mount the machine gun on our left, with which they began to fire at the monks.

The Assault Guards captain, my son's buddy, performed poorly. He was closest to the machine gun but came over to where I was standing to get instructions. I believe I yelled at him.

The rebel soldiers fared better because to fire at them the militias would have needed to fire at us, and maybe they were reluctant to do that because they thought we had saved them from the uprising that morning, at the Hotel Colón. It was only a relative reluctance, though, because gunmen here and there were firing at the monastery door. I ordered the soldiers who were still inside not to come out, and the ones inside the wagons to get down on the floor. The latter obeyed me, but some of the others, thinking their end had come, grabbed their weapons again and fought back. The colonel who had surrendered to me must have been one of them.

The avalanche of people swarming down the sloping street, the name of which I don't remember, broke through the corridor of Guards and knocked me to the ground. It was the first time I have lost my three-cornered hat in close to forty years: I had first put it on when I was eighteen years old, and I was fifty-six when the war began. My uniform ended up looking very disheveled and lost some buttons.

I ordered my captain adjutant to call General Aranguren for reinforcements, and also firemen. I concentrated on trying to stabilize the fighting. This was the first time

I had to fight the internal revolution, and unfortunately not the last. To take over the machine gun nest, we had to inflict losses on the anarchists. A file was opened on each of the Guards that killed them.

Shameful. They didn't dare open a file on me because my support of the government was very recent.

We succeeded in stabilizing the situation when the reinforcements arrived. What the prosecutor says about twenty-five rebel officers having died isn't accurate. We counted only ten, but I don't suppose fifteen one way or the other will change my fate. I insist that the monks fared worse.

I remember one silly detail. Sergeant Bermúdez was very upset at seeing me without my three-cornered hat, and he wouldn't rest until he had found it. When he delivered it to me I didn't want to put it on, and this also affected him a good deal.

I had trouble finding the hesitant colonel. He was badly wounded, and a Guard was holding him in his arms. For whatever consolation it might give him I told him most of his men were safe, and the man thanked me. He could barely talk. I also asked him to forgive me because he had surrendered to me and I couldn't protect him. I remember he said, in just these words, "It's better this way."

He died that same night. He was a very old man, who maybe was no longer in active service and had put on his uniform that day because he thought it was his duty.

The following day, July 20, decided my future. I hadn't been ordered to, but I presented myself at the Generalitat to see President Companys, who saw me right away even though he had so many other obligations at the time. Beforehand I had asked for permission from my general, who said to me, "To resign? There's no procedure in the regulations for us soldiers to resign."

I hadn't used the word "resign". I know the regulations inside out, and it would be very strange for a soldier to have the right to resign in the presence of the enemy. Maybe the reason General Aranguren said "resign" was that, at the time, most Spaniards would have liked to do just that.

In any case, with the indulgence he usually showed me, the general authorized me to tell President Companys whatever was on my mind. It was the general who told me that the president, while we were fighting in Calle Lauria the night before, had met in his office at the Generalitat with anarchists led by Durruti. They were enraged by the death of Ascaso. Those terrible, violent men sat down in front of the president with their rifles between their knees, and Companys apologized for the way the Generalitat had treated the anarchists. He criticized his own party, and he depicted himself as just one more soldier in the fight against fascism. In spite of this information, I went to see him.

Companys was a far better debater than I was. He is one of the cleverest men I've ever known. I started out very angry, and he agreed with everything I said. To calm me down, I remember, he said something that offended me very much: "I understand, Escobar, that what happened in the Carmelite monastery was a great affront to your uniform."

This infuriated me, and I lost my composure. "Mr. President, I'm not a uniform, I'm a man!"

But, even as I was answering him, I remembered that my son had said something similar to me in the Hotel Colón. Ever since José's departure for Italy the pain in and around my heart, down into my left arm, had disappeared completely. It was remarkable.

The president not only wasn't offended by my angry reaction, he praised my attitude. "I wish everybody thought the way you do, Escobar, and didn't fall back on their uniform to justify their behavior. Excuse me for what I said." Well, if you ask me to excuse you, you've disarmed me.

Then he said that if it bothered my conscience to be commanding troops in such a situation, I could be given an administrative assignment. In other words, he offered me—as a favor—the last thing a member of the Civil Guard wants. And that wasn't all, because he proceeded to pass judgment on General Llano de la Encomienda's recent attitude—described it as ambiguous—so I had to come to his defense. I also had to speak up for my general. I was completely buffaloed. I don't know how he did it, but here I had gone to the president's office to accuse him of being soft on anarchy, and I was the one who ended up being on the defensive. So I finally said, in spite of it all, "Excuse me, Mr. President. I think I've made a mistake. But sooner or later you'll have to disarm those men, and then you'll need me and other people who think like me."

"Colonel," he answered, very humbly, "I already need you. I just learned that Cardinal Vidal of Tarragona is being held in the monastery at Poblet by militiamen who are out of control."

~

I took the bait. I'm not saying the president didn't have a clear-cut interest in saving Cardinal Vidal's life, but he offered me the assignment as an incentive, having written me into his book as a *Catholic soldier*.

I'm proud of being a soldier, and I feel very honored to be a Catholic, but not the two things together. That is, I don't like being part of a species within a genus, as if we *Catholic soldiers* formed a separate group. You can see why I feel that way, now that all the soldiers who won the war—which became a Crusade—are Catholics, even some well-known Masons. It's more appropriate to speak of soldiers who are Catholics, or of Catholics who are soldiers. I've explained this to my defense counsel, but I don't know if he has understood it. It's a very important point with me, and I'm going to insist on it by telling a story that, if I tell it well, is even amusing.

In the fall of 1936, after the battle for Madrid, when I went back to Barcelona so Dr. Trueta could finish putting my left arm back together, I saw quite a lot of Manuel Azaña, the president of the Republic, who had settled in to live in the Palace of Pedralbes. I think I've already explained that we got along very well in spite of our major ideological differences, and since I wasn't a politician but a warrior—those words are his—he relaxed and enjoyed kidding me when we talked. Soon after I got to Barcelona Azaña said to me, "They've missed you very much in Catalonia. Especially some of the Church hierarchy."

He was obviously referring to the role I had played in saving the bishops of Tortosa, Gerona, and Barcelona. Since I thought it would be incongruous for me to leave him with the impression that I had settled into fighting alongside the "Reds" to save bishops, I said to President Azaña, very seriously, "I suppose the prostitutes in Chinatown will have missed me more."

I said it deadpan: the few jokes I know how to tell succeed because when I'm telling them, I try to give the impression of being deeply serious. The president looked disconcerted. What I had said could be interpreted as meaning, God save me, that those poor women missed me as a customer.

In reality the episode of the prostitutes I was alluding to was no joke, and when I clarified it for the president, it saddened him. So I regret it. But I just wanted to make the point that I had no desire to end up being a Scarlet Pimpernel for the Spanish clergy. Those first days in Catalonia were full of homicidal insanity, and we tried to protect as many people as possible from it, no matter who they were. And I want to stress that the help I got from Companys in doing that was incalculable.

Now, the episode of the prostitutes was so surreal that when I first read the police report about it I couldn't believe it: street women were being hauled out of Chinatown and shot on the beach at Sitges, on the pretext that they were infecting the soldiers of liberty with venereal disease. I personally researched the facts of the case, which unfortunately turned out to be true, though not on the scale that was attributed to them later. Nor is it at all true that it was Durruti himself who ordered these deeply shameful executions. Our investigation showed it was the doing of a sexually perverted sadist, reputedly a militant in the FAI, who was called "the Lynx". He had a record as a common criminal, and also for rape and attempted rape.

Although it was an appalling story, a string of mistakes made my conversation with the president moderately comical. When I confirmed to him that some executions had taken place, Azaña, horrified, asked me, "But how many did they shoot, Escobar?"

"It's hard to say," I answered. "Many of these poor unfortunate women don't have family to follow up after them." And then I guess I considered it for a moment and said to him, "As it happens, I have a daughter . . . poor girl!"

President Azaña was stunned. He asked me incredulously, "You're saying you have a daughter who's—"

He didn't dare go on, but I saw my clumsiness, and I explained that I was thinking of my daughter Emilia, the Sister of Adoration. Her mission, as part of the mission of her order, is to rescue fallen women. This clarification came as a relief to him. Later he laughed when I told him that the Civil Guard had never had a more enthusiastic reception in Chinatown.

But what I do remember perfectly is the end of the conversation. As I've mentioned, I wanted it to be clear that

I could exercise my independent judgment when it came to saving human lives, so I said to the president, "I'm not saying this to add to your worries but as a precaution. I wouldn't want to go down in history as a colonel who took part in the war just to save bishops—for whom I do, on the other hand, have reverence and respect."

"Do you think you'll go down in history, Escobar?"

I felt I needed to excuse myself for what could be interpreted as presumption. "No, Mr. President, not at all. It was a manner of speaking."

He said to me agreeably, "I hope for your sake you don't go down in history." And then he added bitterly, "But I? Yes, I will go down in history. Or rather . . . I'm afraid I am, already, no more than history."

This last impressed me a great deal.

~

Although I started writing these notes here in this castle-prison Montjuich—I don't know whether as a distraction or out of vanity about my penmanship—I was originally prompted to do it by my fellow prisoners in the prison on the Paseo del Cisne, in Madrid, which is where I went first when I turned myself in at the end of the war. They said to me, "You've lived it all, General, and you should write it down so the truth will be known."

They would be disappointed if they were to read these notes—which they won't, among other reasons because many of them have died—since I don't know what truth can be extracted from them. Besides, I think I only write things that I enjoy remembering, which is natural in my situation. Although what I've written on the previous page seems disrespectful of bishops, it's also true that the subject of Cardinal Vidal, of Tarragona, gave me satisfaction both as a Christian and as a Civil Guard. The reasons for the first are obvious. As for the second, after the deplorable experience at the monastery on Calle Lauria, what we did about the cardinal was organized very well with the help of Colonel Brotons, who was in command of the Rural Division. It was Brotons who confirmed to me that the cardinal had been seized, and that they had already taken him from the monastery at Poblet. We had to act extremely fast because the executions were being carried out very swiftly and in most cases without trial or, if there was one, it was followed immediately by murder. There is no other word for it.

Brotons and I both thought the anarchists would take him to some beach, because we had already heard they'd chosen wild and deserted places like that for their crimes. I took the road to Villanueva y la Geltrú because it was closer to Barcelona, while Brotons went farther south, to Cambrils del Mar. I came upon the party of militia who had the cardinal near Comarruga.

There were two cars, and a lieutenant ordered them to stop so we could make a search. The "responsible" member of the party came up to our officer and invoked the authority of the Committee of Antifascist Militias, which had been established recently. Then I went over to them. The man "responsible" confronted me but not very aggressively, because after our experience in early encounters we deployed quite a few troops as often as we could, being the surest way to avoid clashes. In this case I had two wagons of Guards with me. It's not accurate to say that I'm daring. I make sure I have as much cover as possible. Azaña has written flatteringly about my being daring, but it's not what the Corps regulations prescribe.

Despite the two wagons full of Guards, from one of which a fair number of them emerged and deployed themselves so there would be no doubt about the firmness of our intentions, the "responsible" one pulled out a sheaf of paper scraps in an attempt to show the legality of what he was doing. In cases like this I act on the intuition and instincts that I developed in my long years as a Civil Guard. While the lieutenant was looking over the miscellaneous "papers", I went up to the car holding the cardinal and respectfully bowed to kiss his episcopal ring. He wasn't wearing it, as I had already seen.

I said, "What, Your Eminence? I see they've taken your ring."

Then I turned to face the militiamen. "Tell me, which one of you lot has His Eminence the cardinal's ring?"

One of them, who was wearing a red and black bandana around his neck, stammered out the word "confiscation" but pulled the ring out of his pocket. I took it, put it on the cardinal's ring finger, and kissed it in the usual way.

You can do this only when you have the right cover.

I've mentioned my intuition and instincts as an old Civil Guard because after the moment with the ring, the militiamen were left looking like common horse thieves.

When we transferred the cardinal to my car, the legalistic man who was "responsible" worked up the nerve to ask me, "In whose name are you taking him?"

"In the name of the Generalitat. And you—in whose name were you going to shoot him?"

"We are acting in the name of the Committee of Antifascist Militias, but we weren't going to shoot him"—an attempt to vindicate himself—"we were taking him to be tried."

We were standing on a road that ended at a deserted beach.

"Oh, yes?" I asked. "And where were you going to try him? On that beach?"

The man now didn't know what to say to me. I proceeded with his arrest so the same committee whose authority he invoked could try him. I don't know whether they did.

The war wasn't always painful. It turned out that some situations were entertaining, or at least interesting, as a contrast with the surrounding tragedy. I say that because when I got into my car with the cardinal he thanked me, very effusively, and asked me, "What's happening? Have the soldiers already gotten this far?"

These were very confused times, and he thought he had been saved by the nationalists. I had to clear it up for him: "No, Your Eminence, I'm serving the government of the Republic."

He was so surprised that I was concerned, and I asked him, "Do you think I'm doing the wrong thing?"

I remember that he broke into a smile and told me warmly, "No, my son, you're doing wonderfully!"

Because he thought his enthusiasm seemed excessive, he said by way of excuse, "What can I tell you, son, if you've just saved the life of a prince of the Church, whose willingness to die doesn't match his eminence?"

This last wasn't accurate, because when I went up to the car and he didn't yet know what our intentions were, he gave every appearance of being composed and serene.

I remember Cardinal Vidal y Barraquer as a man of great physical distinction and very agreeable manner.

President Companys helped him leave Spain, and he's lived in Switzerland ever since. He's kept silence this whole time as a rejection of the war and the atrocities committed in it. Even now that it's over, he hasn't wanted to return to Spain, I suppose for the same reason. I think a high-ranking clergyman can express his view in this way. I say that because some people have been amazed that I didn't take advantage of the opportunities I had to leave the country and get away from such a hard and bloody war. But I've always thought that a soldier can't be a soldier unless he's in an army—and that, although war is a horror, if war has to be made we soldiers should make it.

~

I've enjoyed writing the last few pages, but that summer of 1936 was terrible in Barcelona and, from what I've heard since, in the rest of Spain. May God grant that it won't be repeated.

Within the general tragedy I had a private sadness. I left the Corps of the Civil Guard because it went out of existence and was transformed into the National Republican Guard, by order of the government. What a blunder. I had the option of moving to the army, and that's what I did. I was assigned to the Army of the Center.

It's taken the end of the war to make me a Civil Guard

again, but only so I can be tried as a traitor. A lot of consolation that is. During the trial they've let me wear the Corps uniform that, I'll never forget, I first wore when I was only nineteen years old. Now I'm sixty.

Companys very much regretted my leaving Barcelona, and he came to tell me so, because when I joined the Barcelona Urban Division and he had recently become president of the Generalitat, he received me very mistrustfully. We became friends that tragic summer. He decided not to oppose the anarchists openly, but he did grant thousands of passports to families who were in danger. We managed the thing pretty well: although the anarchists controlled the trains and the French border crossings, there were several foreign ships in the harbor and we made a deal with the shipping agents to make passage available. The border guards controlled the port and were very helpful.

The strange thing is that I said good-bye to President Companys as if we were never going to see each other again in this life, yet in a few months I was back in Barcelona. My link with this city is peculiar. I was born in Ceuta, grew up in Valencia, and came to Barcelona at the age of fifty-six thinking it was going to be a temporary assignment. But if the prosecutor has his way it could be my final post.

They posted me to the Talavera front in September of that year, in command of the Móstoles column. This consisted of fifteen hundred men, most of whom had luckily for me been Civil Guards in my Nineteenth Urban Division of Barcelona and had followed me in choosing to join the army.

I'm being tried, as I've said, for my acts against the

Movement on July 19, 1936, but the victors—even my defense counsel—find it incomprehensible that I should have remained in a command in the army during the war. My lawyer, Sierra Valverde, struggles bravely to save my life, and he's hinted more than once, delicately, that the work takes its toll. I've explained to him that I could distinguish between the government of the Republic, which I had sworn an oath to serve, and the ungovernable masses. In my judgment, the rebels are to blame for the masses being ungovernable. He doesn't see it that way and yet despite that defends me very tenaciously, which is all the greater reason for me to be grateful.

When I joined the Army of the Center, the rebels had already set up a military junta in Burgos headed by Major General Cabanellas, whom I remember as having a beard and being a Mason. I'm not one of those who believe the Masons are going directly to hell—which is what Franco seems to think, judging from the courts he's creating to purge them—but I was surprised by the rebels' enthusiastic defense of Catholicism under the leadership of a Mason. And he doesn't seem to have been the worst of them, because I know he interceded, unsuccessfully, to prevent the execution of General Batet, commander of the Sixth Division and therefore General Mola's superior, who was shot just for not having rebelled in 1936. Batet was a friend of mine. He died like a gentleman, calming the soldiers in the firing squad and exonerating them of all blame for carrying out their orders.

I therefore don't believe that in September 1936 there were reasons that would have made me change my decision, at the time of the uprising, about continuing to serve. I was aware that it was now not a matter of a simple military coup, but rather of a civil war with international implications, but I thought it was very possible that it would be short. A vain illusion. In any case I believed, and still believe, that it was better for the armies to be commanded by professionals, prepared to do their work with no more ill will than necessary. When I saw republican troops commanded by leaders like El Campesino, my hair stood on end. My son Antonio arrested El Campesino in Villalba, in the province of Madrid, when Antonio was a lieutenant in the Civil Guard and El Campesino was being sought in the aftermath of the revolution in Asturias in 1934. Later, during the war, when El Campesino was made a colonel, my son Antonio was worried that their paths would cross, because Valentín González had a reputation for holding grudges. When I was promoted to general Antonio said to me, "Well, Father, if El Campesino tracks me down I'll have somebody to fall back on." He said it jokingly, but I believe it took a weight off his mind.

~

I don't know if I've already said that my youngest brother, Alberto, is a bullfighter. Or at least, he was when the war began. Ramón, who after my father's death took over command of the family (with no argument allowed because he was the oldest), was extremely unhappy when Alberto made the decision. Ramón had supposed Alberto would join the Corps, like the rest of us, so Ramón would have authority over him both as his older brother and as his superior in the Corps. That was very characteristic of Ramón, but I take a leaf from his book when I argue with my son Antonio. The truth is that none of us liked Alberto's choice, but afterward we did what we could, without success, to support him in making his bullfighting début in the Monumental, in Madrid. Where he did fight, I believe with young bulls, was in Valencia, thanks to the good connections we had there.

Alberto is the most charming of all the Escobars, although Alfredo's sparkier. I've mentioned Alberto's saying he didn't understand a football match because he was "in the middle of it", which became a byword in the family. I like to record these family stories in the kind of magnificent handwriting you find in a headquarters and headquarters company. Looking back at the early pages, I see it's improving. That's only natural, because it had been a long time since I had any practice. When I was promoted to a command I got a personal assistant who did my writing for me.

Judging from what people say, what I understood least because I was in the middle of it was what I did when I was first assigned to the Army of the Center. I call it an army for lack of a better term, but in reality it was a hard-to-describe grab bag of people's militias. Although at the end of September Largo Caballero's government issued a decree requiring their integration into the army, the order wasn't carried out because the anarchists couldn't understand the need for a regular, uniformed military.

I feel bad about saying how much this pained me, but it wasn't out of any spirit of militarism. It was because those poor men were being mowed down in the attacks by the professionals of the Army of Africa commanded by General Yagüe. I felt that instead of fighting the enemy, my job—and that of my men who came from the Civil Guard—was to save the lives of our soldiers, some of them volunteers but others who had been forced into serving. This was a real torment for me because they were very young kids who would even cry when the Moors attacked. Many of them would therefore just turn and run, and we had try to restore order as much to avoid more losses as to contain the enemy. These were very tense moments, when our front would crumble away and we would have to hold our men together with jokes. It seems that I would harangue them with a sentence that acquired some notoriety: "It's not that you shouldn't run when you see the enemy, just that it's safer if you can do it without turning your back on them."

It might be true that I said it, because it fits with my basic concept of retreat in the face of the enemy. What I don't remember is actually closing with or shooting at that enemy, though President Azaña has written that my conduct in the attack at Navalcarnero was heroic, or exemplary. I don't remember exactly what he said because the president himself read it to me from a book he's writing. He also commented, with that bitterness that left such a bad taste in my mouth, "But don't expect that anybody'll thank you for it, Escobar, or repay you one bit."

"It's enough for me that you say it, Mr. President," I replied with all my heart, for it was a great honor for me to be received by and talk privately with the head of state. I remember that my father, when he had just been promoted to major, was received in a general audience at the palace by the queen regent, María Cristina, in which he had occasion to kiss the hand of the sovereign and she addressed a few words to him. My father recounted it to us several times very reverently, which was natural because he never thought a citizen of such humble origin could attain such a height. I don't think it had anything to do with vanity. My father had none of that. But it would have made him proud to know that his son rose, from being just a corporal at the time of my father's death, to being singled out that way by the first magistrate of the nation.

Azaña was very congenial and spoke very compellingly, but he would always throw in a finishing touch of bitterness. Especially after the war had spread through the whole country. I knew him from before, when he was minister of war and I had the job of providing a security detail as he moved here and there.

But I repeat, I don't know how an action can be called heroic that consists entirely of ordering a retreat, without even seeing the face of the enemy. Of course, we didn't have any option.

This is how, having lost Talavera, we got as best we could to Madrid, where Rojo had planned that we would engage Yagüe and Mola's armies.

~

It was in Madrid that I met Lieutenant Colonel Rojo for the first time and our friendship began. Although General Miaja was the chairman of the Madrid Defense Council, we as professionals knew that Rojo was its true mastermind. The government had decamped, out of political prudence, to Valencia, except for President Azaña, who moved to Barcelona. I've never understood that point very well, but I wasn't such a confidant of his that I could ask him why.

When I entered the capital through the Extremadura pass and we reached the slope of Campo del Moro, my heart sank. The city was full of posters featuring the hammer and sickle, an allusion to the Soviet Union, and large portraits of La Pasionaria, which were what made her famous. A very great sadness came over me, and it was one of the moments when I wondered whether I had made the right choice.

When we got to the junction with the Gran Vía, we had to stop the car to let a column of the International Brigades march past. People were cheering them, thinking they would save us. The sight of these young men discouraged me even more, because the way they marched didn't suggest they would be great fighters. When my brother Alberto used to torture us with his bullfighting sessions in the living room, he would say, "You know whether somebody's a bullfighter or not by the way he takes hold of the cape." He said he took hold of it very well. Well, these boys were carrying their rifles as if they were brooms.

Sergeant Bermúdez was driving the car, and to protect his status as a driver he managed to spend the entire war without being promoted to sergeant first class. Needless to say, he needed my complicity to bring it off. We had grown accustomed to each other. He sometimes writes me letters that gladden my heart. If he's demobilized in time he'll try to come and see me. My lawyer says they'll lift my solitary confinement when my sentence is final.

I was saying that Sergeant Bermúdez was driving the car, and when we stopped to let the International Brigades column pass, he said, "Do you think these foreigners are worth anything, Colonel?"

This shrewd buck sergeant, who knew my thought processes, said it to flatter me or raise a smile. But this time he didn't get one, and in fact very much the opposite happened: I felt the pain around my heart and the pins and needles it caused—something that doesn't happen to me in the heat of battle—because most of the men were very young and would have mothers and fathers who would never see them again. You didn't need to be a fortuneteller to know that many of them would be buried in our soil forever. A girl went up to one who reminded me of José—I sometimes think any young man reminds me of José—and gave him a kiss. His comrades laughed, and he blushed. It was pitiful to see how he carried his gun. He looked as if he might fire it any moment.

I was very discouraged when I arrived at Miaja's headquarters, and I got angry with a soldier-typist who, without lifting his eyes from the typewriter, told me Lieutenant Colonel Rojo wasn't seeing anybody. It wasn't the personal offense, but how far army discipline had fallen. Of course, as soon as Rojo learned I was there he saw me right away and gave me his full attention, unfailingly using the forms of address that were appropriate for me as his superior even though I was subject to his orders because he was chief of the general staff of the Madrid

Defense Council. Dealing with such a man made up for a good deal of turmoil and frustration.

We eyed each other with curiosity. We soldiers all think this war boiled down to a face-off between Rojo and Franco. Both of them are excellent strategists.

I remember that when we began our conversation Rojo offered me a cigar, which I declined because I didn't smoke, and he asked me for permission to light his. His hands were plump, his face was very pale, and he had a mustache and wore very round glasses. He was of average height. He didn't seem like a man who would be at home in open country, but he once visited the Madrid front on horseback. He didn't have a rider's posture. The most graceful horseman I've known was General Aranguren. Shortly before the end of the war he injured his leg in a fall from a horse in Valencia, where he was the commandant of the fort. That injury, I've been told, was the reason he had to be sitting in a chair when they shot him. This kind of information always gets through to you, I'm not sure how, even if you're in solitary confinement.

I admired the way Rojo got right down to business. When I said, at the start, that I considered myself subject to his orders, he corrected me politely by saying I was subject to Miaja's. I clarified that I meant in matters of strategy, and that prompted him to share an important confidence with me. He told me he was sure that November 10—this was on November 8, 1936; there are some dates you don't forget—the nationalists under General Varela would attack via the Casa de Campo and try to advance along the Manzanares, to create a bridgehead between the Montaña barracks and Modelo Prison. If they succeeded, they would be able to enter Madrid. He explained this to me on a map.

"I'm not saying this because I have the intuition of a strategic genius," he said, "but because last night we captured a nationalist officer who was carrying a detailed plan of the campaign."

That's when he took me into his confidence and showed me the plan he had gotten from the enemy. He could have given me the orders that followed without making such a confidential explanation, although it's true that, once I knew how important my mission was, I put my all into it.

Although I could see he felt the urgency of wrapping up my orders, he could still take time to turn to a topic that was seemingly unrelated to his job. That's what he did when, to my great surprise, he praised my performance at Escalona, which wasn't very different from what it had been at Navalcarnero or Talavera. To find out what lay behind his unexpected compliments I made a quip. "Look, Rojo, at Escalona I felt like a Civil Guard trying to bring a stampede of strikers under control."

I was glad because I made him laugh, and during those days we had very little occasion for that. It also gave him a chance to follow up on his subject. "Slowing down that stampede," he said, "gave the International Brigades time to get to Madrid."

"Do you think they're that important?"

"They've raised the morale of the people. They think democratic, civilized Europe is on our side. But yes, the brunt of the battle will fall on the people's militias, and you already know them well. They're willing to die defending their street corner, but they run when they're in the open field."

He then gave me my mission. To cut off the foreseeable stampede by the militias, I was to place myself with my column where the bulk of Varela's forces would attack, at the east wall of the Casa de Campo.

He said, very insistently, "You're going to have to be very tough."

Taking advantage of my deafness, I replied by asking him to clarify. "With whom?"

He looked as though he didn't understand my question, so I repeated, "With whom? With our own army?"

"That's right, Colonel."

"You should understand, Rojo, that since the uprising began I've had hardly any chance to fight the rebels."

"Don't worry, Colonel, you'll have a lot of chances. This is going to be a very long war."

He said it quite calmly, because he was more of a soldier than I was, and at the end of the day, he had prepared himself for the profession of war and I had not. I reflected unhappily on that and remembered that this wasn't a war we had begun.

He went on to take another one of his detours, although in this case it really did have nothing to do with the mission. Vicente Rojo was a Catholic like me, very observant, and he suffered from the confusion that the uprising had created on that key subject. So he took his detour to air the subject with someone he knew shared his view of it. His natural calm broke when he talked about it, and he accused Franco, Aranda, Mola, and so forth, of having appropriated our religion. He mentioned almost everybody who commanded the nationalist armies and told me which ones were Masons. I won't repeat the list because in my circumstances I shouldn't pass judgment offhand. I felt free earlier to mention that General Cabanellas, the head of the Burgos junta, was a Mason because that was notorious.

This hijacking of religion prompted our troops to think, when they were attacked by the rebels under banners flaunting the cross, that they were being assaulted hy the emissaries of Christ. And that in turn exacerbated the anticlericalism in our zone, which was already strong enough without any further stimulus. I don't think this can be good for the religion in whose embrace I want to die—sooner rather than later, I'm afraid—even though all the victors, now, are Catholics.

We got a lot off our chest, both of us, talking about these things. Going on along the lines I've described, Rojo told me about a confrontation he had had that summer with Castro Delgado, a Communist who at the time was in command of the legendary Fifth Regiment. In their argument, Rojo confessed publicly that he was a Catholic through and through even though he was serving a legally constituted government with which, from a Catholic point of view, he couldn't agree. Castro yelled at him, "You should be on their side! This means the leaders of our own side are against us! What chaos this is, sir."

While we were on this subject, which we had so very few chances to talk about, Rojo told me I would have to risk my life in the days ahead. I asked him therefore to suggest a priest who could confess me.

"The simplest thing," he said, "would be to go to the Salesian school."

"But is it still operating as a school?" I was surprised.

"No, it's operating as a barracks, but it's being protected by the Red Youth Guards."

Things like this happen in wars, and I had the chance to look into this one personally because I took his advice and went to the school, in Atocha Circle. A regiment of Youth Guards was in fact quartered there and living with the Salesian fathers. Apparently the latter had a good reputation among the workers because of the scholarships they granted to their children. Maybe this was an arbitrary or very personal reason to protect them, but it consoled me to know there was a possibility of such an understanding, even if it was very precarious.

~

The next day I went to war on the Metro. We got on at Atocha Station and transferred to the Opera Line at Sol.

Since my men were going on foot I didn't want to sit, and I held on to a bar overhead. I was very uncomfortable, because most of us deaf people are put off-balance by the metallic sound of wheels on rails. Sergeant Bermúdez, disgruntled because they had taken away his car, commented, "I get the feeling I'm going not to the front, Colonel, but to the movies." Apparently, when he lived in Madrid he took the Metro only to go to the movies in the Gran Vía.

I played deaf, which didn't take much effort under the circumstances, and he repeated, raising his voice, "It just doesn't seem serious to take the Metro to go to war!"

It might not have been serious, but it was safer because

the enemy was shelling the area around the viaduct. Besides which, these were the days of unlimited nationalist bombing, which also affected the civilian population and which I don't want to get into here. On the other hand, I look back on that trip on the Metro and my conversations with Sergeant Bermúdez with pleasure. When he showed his disagreement with making war on the Metro, I said, "Well, so put your complaint in writing as per regulations."

I've already explained that the few jokes I know how to make involve being very serious, which requires very little effort because I have a forbidding face. Sometimes I succeed in disconcerting the person I'm talking to, as I did in this case. Bermúdez looked worried and begged my pardon.

I've said I remember that trip with pleasure, but also with melancholy. The cars we were in weren't in a special convoy but just part of a normal train that was carrying all sorts of civilians, even women and children. The latter were enjoying themselves, poor things. Some militiamen foolishly took out their pistols for them to touch. I never allowed this when I was present.

People were seeking refuge on the platforms, as the safest place to ride out the nationalist bombings that I don't want to get into but were an outrage. I'm sure they had an influence on our rear guard's reprisals, which were another outrage. The Marxist militants took advantage of the fact that people were gathered in these improvised shelters to hold their meetings there. I've always thought that people who talked so much didn't have time to go to the front. I've also always thought that people who talked so much, on both sides, were the ones responsible for the war. There weren't too many of them, but they made a lot of noise. They say now that the war was inevitable. Which of course they are going to say after they've caused such a disaster. It's worth mentioning that, on our side, this provocation was welcomed by the revolutionaries, who used it as the pretext they needed to mount a revolution, with so much chaos and cruelty that it was criminal recklessness to join in. I don't believe I ever stopped fighting, even for one second, both against the nationalist rebellion and against the revolution. We succeeded in ending the revolution in 1937. The nationalist rebellion was ended by the people who say they've been purified by their victory.

If I don't at least say what I believe and believe what I say, I don't see the point of having gone through so much, or of dying in the way that seems so likely.

By taking streets that were protected from enemy fire, it was easy to get from Opera Station to our assigned position. My observation post was very well situated, and I quickly understood the magnitude of the attack heading our way. With my faint hearing, I've kept my excellent eyesight. Even at my age I'm writing this without glasses, and I've been just as lucky with my distance vision. I therefore could make out, through binoculars, the nationalist trucks approaching along the Extremadura road, full of Carlist troops in their red berets and yellow tassels. It was the first time I had seen them or their banners with religious motifs, which I've already mentioned. The green of the Legion, the red fezzes of the regular troops, the turbans of the Moors, all stood out against the bare patches of woods around the Casa de Campo, and I could make out the supporting Italian and German tanks that would inflict so much suffering on us during the war.

I don't know why I'm writing these pages unless it's because I've always had a passion for penmanship, which I've hardly been able to practice because of the rootless life I've led, a soldier's life. I sometimes dream that my cell, in its forced and almost welcome solitude, is the cell of a Carthusian monk (it's austere enough for that), and that I'm making up for my rootlessness now. But I'm not writing out of any desire to tell war stories, just as my father before me never wanted to tell us his, though they were very remarkable. And if he ever did mention them to us it was to teach us something from them, although at the end of his life you could see his skepticism growing, without affecting his good humor. So when he left for Cuba for the last time at the end of 1897, he said goodbye to us with an especially heartfelt feeling, because everybody knew that the war he was going to, against the powerful Americans, made no sense. When he said goodbye to us he emphatically urged Ramón and me, as his eldest sons, to enlist in the Civil Guard, a very honorable and distinguished Corps, as being more rewarding and not requiring travel or war service. And so we did, although that last point hasn't been borne out.

I don't want to tell war stories, but the reason I just told one, above, is that the enemy made a very colorful impression on me, compared to the figure we cut—even my Guards—in our dull dun uniforms. We were the very picture of misery.

Behind us, the militiamen kept on digging our trenches.

Women were helping them, and children were playing on the mounds of sand as if they were at the beach. I personally ordered them to take away the children, and one woman asked me, very respectfully, "Let them play a little, sir. We'll take them away when the war begins."

I was moved by her innocent idea that advance notice is given of a war's beginning.

~

My sector of the front stayed calm that day, as Rojo had told me it would, and my son Antonio visited me wearing his National Republican Guard uniform. We hadn't seen each other since the beginning of the war. He had been serving in the rear guard in University City, and when he heard I had arrived in Madrid it wasn't hard for him to find me. July 18 had caught him in the capital.

I hadn't had time to see any of my family in Madrid, and he told me about all of them. I had the chance to see them later. He gave me the news—I don't know whether it was good or bad, but anyway it saddened me—that my brother Alfredo had holed up in the Mexican embassy. He was in command of a division of the Civil Guard when the uprising happened, and he stayed in that post so he wouldn't have to participate in the assault on the Montaña barracks. Antonio told me, maybe to excuse his uncle Alfredo, that assault had been very brutal.

I tried to hide my dismay and concentrated on Antonio's situation, warning him—trying not to betray Rojo's confidence—that the next day would bring the brunt of the enemy attack. I asked him where he would be, and instead of answering he said, "I won't be with you, Father. My superiors have encouraged me to apply for a transfer to your column, but I can't stand the idea of being in combat with you, thinking that something might happen to you and I wouldn't have been able to take care of you."

Seeing my silence, his voice broke in a way that was unbecoming in a career officer, and he asked me, "Do you think that's bad, Father?"

"I think it's fine, son, because that way I won't have the responsibility of taking care of you."

I find it such a pleasure, in these closing days, to record family things. Antonio went into the Assault Guards when the security forces were reorganized, and when Catalonia fell he was posted in Barcelona. That's why he, too, is a prisoner here in this castle Montjuich. Coincidences like these are the fortunes of life. Luckily, the prosecutor is seeking only a prison sentence for him. A long sentence, but I think life is wonderful even in this cell. If I don't share my lawyer's eagerness to save my life, it's not because I don't value it but rather because I think it's a futile effort.

The commanding officer of the sector was Colonel Alzugaray, and I asked him by field telephone for permission to be absent from my position for a couple of hours. He was surprised, but he gave it to me because I had the reputation of fulfilling my obligations.

We again took the Metro, despite Sergeant Bermúdez's objections, to go to the Mexican embassy on Calle Orfila. It was still the safest way to travel. Two other Guards came along as my escort. There weren't many people out and about at that hour and I took a seat. In a little while a woman got on at one of the stops, and I got up to give her my seat. "Never mind, never mind," the lady said to me. "You must be tired."

It seemed important to me, in such sad and extraordinary circumstances, to do the things of ordinary life and not let a lady stand while I sat. Some people would think this foolish, but we Escobars, with all our defects, have always behaved courteously, the first among us being my father, who nobody would say came from a village of illiterate peasants.

At the embassy I had to prove that my brother was taking refuge there in order to be admitted myself. I walked into a different world, an oppressed world that oppressed me as I followed the functionary who led me through the hallways—which didn't seem like hallways because of the mattresses that were laid out in them—and through the large, beautifully decorated salons that had been converted into improvised kitchens, with little alcohol burners that heated faint-smelling broths. When I was walking through these places, the refugees looked at me with natural mistrust and even hatred, because I represented the enemy that had forced them into being shut up there if they wanted to save their lives. I, who was fighting to be nobody's enemy. A vain illusion.

My brother Alfredo's room was big, with at least six beds in it, but when I entered the room their occupants left so we could be by ourselves. We didn't hesitate even for a moment to embrace each other warmly. How thin Alfredo was! I almost didn't recognize him at first. It was such a joy to see him. He was my little brother, and (I hope Ramón will forgive me) I was the one who bestirred myself to start him out on the track of a career officer, although then all of us made the sacrifices necessary to make it possible. We were sure he would be the only one to make general, and we weren't wrong because when the war began he was already a lieutenant colonel even though he was eight years younger than I. Well, the war has turned everything upside down.

His thinness surprised me because I had supposed that our sister Amelia—about whom I wish I had time to say more—would have been bringing him food. He confirmed that she was, but that it had to be shared among many. He meant his fellow refugees. I scolded him for his generosity. To interrupt my reprimand, I think, he asked me with his very characteristic facetiousness, "So . . . what are you up to that you're not in the war?"

I barely had time to laugh because, inevitably, we got into an argument. The subject of it came up right away. He immediately said he considered himself freed from his oath to the constitution, and that he would cross over to the other zone as soon as he could to fight alongside Franco, his classmate at the academy. I don't know if this latter circumstance influenced his decision. What I do know is that if Alfredo told me he considered himself freed from his oath, it was because he believed it in all conscience.

Even though we kept our voices low on account of where we were, we couldn't avoid getting a little heated during our argument, and at one point Alfredo told me, "I'm going to do the same thing your son José's done."

He said it with no bad intention, as a point of argument, but that was how I found out that my youngest son had succeeded in returning from Italy to enlist in Franco's army. I was the last to know. My son Antonio also knew it, but he didn't want to tell me because he didn't want me to be upset. And Alfredo told me only in the heat of argument, or inadvertently, so when he saw I was upset he didn't know how to beg my pardon or console me. The tingling in my arm, which I had almost forgotten since the war began, started up again.

"Don't worry, Antonio, nothing'll happen to him. You'll see," Alfredo repeated several times, not just to make me feel better but also to convince himself that the war would last just a matter of days. He and his fellow fugitives were keeping their spirits up with the prospect of the immediate entry of Mola's troops into Madrid, as was being announced by the nationalist radio these unfortunate men listened to with such devotion every night. That was why Alfredo showed more concern about what might happen to me, when this expectation was corroborated, than he did about his own situation.

In the end we struggled over money. I offered him what I had on me, because he was going to need it to cross over into the other zone, but he insisted I would need it more than he would. That was how sure he was that Madrid would change zones in a matter of hours. I laugh when I look back on it, because we were no longer arguing heatedly but making careful judgments about who would need the money more.

He finally accepted it, not because he was convinced but out of respect for his older brother.

I saw only the beginnings of the battle for Madrid, because I was wounded on the night of November 10. Lieutenant Colonel Rojo had told me that if the enemy attack didn't succeed in carrying our position that day, they wouldn't be able to form a bridgehead between the Montaña barracks and Modelo Prison. And that would mean that, having worn out their main contingent, they would have to give up on their entry into Madrid. He supported it with so many reasons and said it with such assurance that I had no choice but to put my faith in it wholeheartedly.

During the day, as we had expected, we had to hold back deserting militiamen and get them to go back on the attack, sometimes with reasoning and sometimes by force. This was very risky for us, because they thought we were protected in the rear and we were sending them to their deaths. Many of my Guards had to join them in counterattacks and lost their lives doing it. I can't forget them. They were fathers of families and never understood politics.

The militiamen were especially afraid of the tanks, until we could show them that in wooded country they were of less use and more vulnerable, because if we managed to explode a hand grenade in their tracks they were good for nothing. I think it was one of the first battles to see the use against these armored vehicles of what have come to be called Molotov cocktails.

The sector commander, Colonel Alzugaray, advised General Miaja of the losses suffered by my column. The general called me on the field telephone to buck me up, which I certainly needed, and to tell me that he was sending us the Cordoba Battalion and the Fifth Mixed Brigade to reinforce us. I thanked him and emphasized the urgency of doing so, saying that without them I thought I would be fighting in the streets of Madrid. I remember that General Miaja, who was affable and optimistic by nature, said to me, "Don't worry, Escobar, that won't happen."

Just out of habit, I answered, "May the Lord God hear you."

"You seem to forget," the general said jokingly, "that God's on their side, not on ours."

It's odd, but I can hear pretty well on a field telephone, through my left ear, of course. It was the sort of joke I had never liked much, so I answered Miaja by asking, "Do you believe, General, that God takes sides in a war?"

"That's what *they* say," General Miaja replied. He never let up on a joke once he got it going. I think I've said Miaja didn't have much luck with the jokes he made to me, but it was his way.

Lieutenant Colonel Rojo called me on the phone at the end of the afternoon. He bucked me up in another way. He told me the enemy had suffered much greater losses than we had, and that what they hadn't done that day they wouldn't be able to do the next. He was completely assured, which is what I've always thought made him a great strategist. He told me our position was right at the point of the attack, under Varela, that was aimed at establishing one of the three bridges over the Manzanares, which would have opened their way to the Palace of Moncloa.

Night fell and we fought on, sometimes hand to hand, and it was then that they wounded me. I don't know how because I lost so much blood that I quickly passed out.

In my trial, the prosecutor has elaborated on the main charge by referring to the *coincidence* of my being in Madrid with the very people in our rear guard who were committing the greatest excesses, culminating in the killings at Torrejón and Paracuellos that have come to light since then. Because the prosecutors have so many cases to deal with, they investigate them very hurriedly, so my prosecutor has gathered from investigating mine that my role during the war was to subdue the rear guard and enforce public order. That conclusion laid him open to a very successful stroke by my counsel, who with just a few questions showed that on those dates I didn't belong to the security forces but rather to the army—and that, specifically, when so many lives were unjustly snuffed out, my own was in grave danger at the Ritz Hotel, which had been converted into a military hospital. The anarchist Durruti died in that same hospital during those same days, from bullet wounds he had sustained at the front. We had both been in Barcelona on July 19, in the fight against the rebels, and now again we were both on the Madrid front, with the difference that he died like a hero and I saved my life to die as God wills I must.

Contrary to what has been said, I'm not aware of having had a relationship or any exchange of opinions with Durruti. Not because of any disrespect to him personally, but out of disagreement with his aims, which I thought were very damaging to our country. The Catalan militias, I'm sorry to have to say, were among the most terrified, unmanageable troops during the first days of the battle for Madrid, although their leader, Durruti, later cleansed the stain of their disgrace with his blood.

It seems to me that whenever I talk about the anarchists I judge them harshly, and given that my life is in such a precarious situation I should be careful about such judgments. I say I didn't talk to Durruti, but I did talk, very gladly and honorably, with Melchor Rodríguez García, who also was an anarchist, very old and battle-hardened. He was put in charge of prisons at the end of that year 1936 and acted so energetically and bravely, risking his own life, that he succeeded in shutting down in a very few days the indiscriminate killings perpetrated by his like-minded believers, and the very calculated ones of the Communists. In Madrid, at least. It very much comforts me to see what the honor and courage of a lone man can accomplish. I need that comfort because in it I seek my own consolation, having felt very lonely throughout this war, and even though the people who judge me most mercifully consider me to be a dreamer who would have done better to leave the country. Melchor didn't want to flee either, and I know that at the end of the war he was the mayor of Madrid. I don't know what might have become of him.

I had two wounds: one that the doctors thought would be mortal because a bullet had penetrated deep into my chest, and another one that was less serious but, because it broke my left arm, had longer-lasting aftereffects. I don't doubt the doctors' judgment, and if I didn't die on an occasion that would have done me so much honor, it was because God wills me to die without it.

They had to put me through several operations, and I was unconscious for seven days, in a sleep that wasn't always painful, as happens with anesthesia, because I had dreams. I sometimes even saw my wife and my children when they were small and we would take them on country excursions in the spring. I saw my wife very clearly, and I could tell that she was looking at me very intently, paying close attention to everything that was happening to me, which I myself was unaware of. I also saw my son José, with great relief, because he wasn't armed or wearing his blue shirt but just appeared as a young boy playing with his sister, Emilia. I saw her a few times in her novice's habit and at other times in her usual clothes. My son Antonio was the only one I saw as he really was, in a uniform that I didn't recognize because the National Republican Guard uniform had been adopted very recently. I mean that I saw him as he really was, although I didn't know it, because when I was wounded both Rojo and General Miaja himself relieved Antonio of any duty that would take him elsewhere. Other members of the family also visited me, but there is no point in recording obvious details.

Later Antonio told me how in my delirium I had jumbled a lot of things together but was always obsessively asking whether it was nighttime. He would say to me, "Yes, Father," to calm me down, because I would feel better when he said it. I do see a clear explanation for this obsession, which was nothing more than my desire to accomplish the mission I had been given, thinking I would have done that if I hadn't been dislodged from my position by the time night fell. I was obsessed to the point that it was the first question I asked Antonio as soon as I recovered my senses. When he explained to me that our defenses had held and the enemy had been stopped at the gates of Madrid, I felt I don't know what strange sensation because it was sad that doing my duty would mean stretching out a war in which my beloved son José, and soon my brother Alfredo, would be facing me on the other side. In my weakness, extreme as it was, I felt lost to sadness.

I strangely felt I knew the face of the woman leaning over me, which in my dreams I began to confuse with that of my wife. The face belonged to the nurse who was taking care of me, and when I was myself again I was so sure I knew her that I addressed her in the familiar form of *tú*, something I never did with a woman I didn't know. I think she was the first person I asked, "Aren't I dead?"

I asked it in all seriousness, but my son Antonio, who was there, thinking that one of the senses I had recovered was my sense of humor, answered, "Not yet, Father." So —according to Antonio—I asked the nurse, "Then who are you (*tú*)?" She didn't answer, and Antonio answered for her, "She's your nurse, Father. You've confused her with an angel, so you think you've died."

Antonio, too, likes to crack jokes. Everybody in our family tries to crack jokes.

It was a long convalescence. It lasted until Christmas, and I got to the point where I forgot we were in a war. Although on our side we said we were fighting for equality among the social classes, the truth is that I was in a private room, a great privilege that I didn't protest, at first because I didn't have the strength to do so and later because Magdalena continued to look after me there, and I soon began to feel a natural affection for her. Magdalena is the nurse I met in my dreams. She was forty-two years old and had blonde hair that she always wore up. She was careful to keep her white uniform in pristine condition, and given my appreciation of uniforms this was another reason to be attracted to her. Her face was very appealing, with a touch of color. She spoke in such a low voice that, until I explained about my deafness, I could barely understand her. So, in order not to intrude on the quiet that the place required, she would lean over my left ear—which is the good one, or the less bad one—and whisper. Having her so near to me, I noticed a distinct emotion, which I found disturbing because I sometimes thought that, in my retirement, having fulfilled my obligations to my children, I could take vows as a religious brother in the order of which I was, or am, a tertiary. And although those disturbing feelings weren't the slightest bit sinful, neither were they appropriate in a monk-to-be, and even less so in a monk who on that November 14, four days after being wounded, turned fifty-seven by the express will of God. For I repeat that, according to the surgeon who removed the bullet from my lung, I should have died.

I feel awkward saying it, but when I regained my strength thanks to the blood transfusions they gave me, I was seized by a great desire to live. The people looking after me avoided giving me any war news in the early stages of my convalescence, to avoid slowing it down. I got used to not hearing about the war and then lost interest in it because I was more interested in everything that involved Magdalena. I've always had trouble sleeping and would wake up at dawn, which I now was especially looking forward to, regretting that in the winter it would be so long in coming. When it did come, Magdalena would come into my room to start giving me the care I needed.

She always maintained the same composure and attention to her dress, and you could hardly notice the fatigue in her face—which looked more lovely to me every day—even when she had stayed awake all night. That happened often, because although I tried to forget about the war, she continued to meet her obligations, and there was a lot of work to do in the hospitals. It was so tiring that, one day when Magdalena was taking my temperature, she excused herself, sat down on a chair that had no back, and immediately fell asleep. Looking at her, I was moved and no doubt in love, because I again and again tried to work out the difference between our ages, since I hadn't yet found out exactly how old she was. I thought I was younger than my chronological age, because I had always led the well-ordered life of a soldier. At least, so I imagined.

Although she had a very pleasant manner, Magdalena was a woman of few words. But she did let me know that she wasn't actually a nurse by profession. I was tempted for a moment to ask Sergeant Bermúdez—he came to visit me almost every day—to find out about her, which would have been a simple thing to do because of the experience we have in the Corps in doing things like that. But I'm glad I didn't ask him.

Her hands were delicate, like those of a person unaccustomed to manual or at least hard labor. Although she spoke so little, the way she spoke was very restrained and polished, and seeing that she had no great interest in politics I wondered what her reasons were for being a volunteer nurse in the war. Until I decided not to worry about it any more and just to enjoy my enforced rest, glad to have such welcome company. Any time she was late in coming to my room, I worried that she might have been assigned to work somewhere else.

Her lilting accent suggested she was from Andalusia, which she was, from Cordoba as she told me. We didn't have many chances to talk because she had so much work to do, as I've explained. We had more chances when my rehabilitation began, because it was her job at the beginning to get me out of bed and into a wheelchair, then into a chair, and later to get me back up and walking.

Out of consideration for her, and for my own privacy, I forced myself from the start to get out of bed by myself, to save her from having to help me in such an intimate way.

This situation lasted barely a month, and it seemed to me the longest and most fulfilling time in the war. While it continued, I forgot I was serving a government whose ideology I couldn't share and was caught up in a war fighting against my son José and my brother Alfredo. This situation seemed so absurd to me that I dreamt of its being set right and of peace being restored. I didn't know how such a miracle might come to pass, but it would have to do so if I were going to establish a legitimate relationship with this woman to whom I didn't think I was indifferent. What I did determine was that she wasn't married.

~

When what I'm writing gives me pleasure, I write quickly and effortlessly. That was true of what I've just written. As I go along in these notes I'm afraid I get distracted from my personal recollections and let down my comrades from Cisne Prison, in Madrid, where I was first held. They were the ones who got me going in writing them, so the truth would be known. What truth?

I face the truth that interests me now with the priest who looks after me. Fortunately, they now let me go to Mass every day. I remember that I was posted in Madrid when my son Antonio was posted as a lieutenant in Villalba, and we rented a house to spend the very hot Madrid summer there and get some relief from the heat, especially at night, by being near the Guadarrama. Although I wasn't a lady's man in the bad sense of that term, I did take some care about my appearance, and it was important for a Civil Guard to have a mustache with upturned points, which we would preserve by sleeping with a mustache guard. This was such a preoccupation with me that on Sunday, the only day of the week that I would step into a church, I didn't take off the mustache guard until the last minute, which would make me late for Mass, to the annoyance of my wife. She would scold me, very rightly, for such vanity. I wasn't very pious at the time.

When I became a widower, in my loneliness and the unforgettable sadness of suddenly losing two children to unknown illnesses, I was disoriented and came to believe that the hand of God had let go of me. That wasn't so, and I got to know the Franciscan fathers on Calle Ferraz, in Madrid. Saint Francis of Assisi was also a soldier, and although he wasn't an outstanding one he did, like me, have to take part in making war. I took an interest in his life and he in mine. That's what I believe, and I continually ask him to help me in what there is of mine that's left to me.

The Franciscan fathers did me a lot of good. They've tried to visit me now, and I've tried to prevent them because it wouldn't be good for them to have a relationship with me during these days. For the same reason, I haven't wanted my brother Ramón, much less Alfredo, to visit me.

Although I was a practicing Catholic when I was relatively young, I didn't meet the Franciscan fathers until 1932, and yet I'm regarded on the republican side as carrying my religion to extremes. So much so that even President Azaña, when he had occasion to, confided in me on the subject.

I say I don't get tired of writing what I take pleasure in remembering, so on these short winter days the twilight catches me with pen in hand, which I have to put aside when it gets dark because the light bulb gives such inadequate light and is so badly placed that it wouldn't allow me to enjoy the shapes of the letters. So, following the advice I've been given, I try to read edifying books. I also reread, and with particular pleasure, the books that taught me how to write at the academy in Getafe when I was a young Civil Guard.

On the other hand, I've politely asked the commandant of the castle not to give me any more magazines or newspapers, because instead of distracting me they leave me completely unsettled. Reading Saint John of the Cross also unsettles me sometimes, but in that case I succeed, albeit with effort, in extracting something of value for what I expect lies in store for me soon. All I get out of the unsettling things I read in the newspapers and magazines, though, is anger, and that's a luxury I can't allow myself.

~

The first time they let me leave the hospital during my rehabilitation was on December 24, 1936, which, even though it was Christmas Eve, stupidly wasn't a holiday on our side. But my son Antonio—who had been relieved of the duty of caring for me and had by then resumed his combat duties, which were very hard during those days in Boadilla del Monte—told me later how, spontaneously, hostilities were suspended for a few hours. The English members of the International Brigades sang their Christmas carols from the trenches, and our soldiers responded with our *villancicos*. But since the *villancicos* were common to both sides, there were moments when both trenches joined in. I know this doesn't amount to anything, but the fact that the two sides could agree on something, if only for a short time, consoles me.

That afternoon, I confess, I was pretty consoled in general because Magdalena came with me on my first walk, and since I didn't know whether she was required to do it as part of her work or she did it of her own accord, I thought what I liked and was happy.

My hospital was the most luxurious hotel in Madrid, unthinkable for a Civil Guard on a modest salary except in my circumstances. It was located in the most beautiful neighborhood in Madrid, next to the church of Los Jerónimos, where the kings of Spain were married when we had them, and near the Retiro Park, which is known everywhere. We were so close to the park that, even though I couldn't walk much, we could get as far as the central pond, which was of average size. It was frozen over because that year cold was added to the inevitable sufferings of the war. The neighborhood was so quiet that we could dream we were in a period of peace. I remember that in one little plaza some children were helping a woman collect wood from some ancient trees, and a man had climbed one of the trunks and was cutting branches with an ax. The scene was the very picture of neediness, but in my eyes it was one of a country family preparing their Christmas Eve dinner. That was how much pleasure I took in being alive.

To start a conversation on a personal note as we were walking up the little rise that leads to the pond, I said, "My family's spread out across a country at war, fighting each other, and yet it's the first Christmas Eve in many years that I don't feel particularly sad."

"But aren't you cold?" she said, as if that were her only concern about me.

"I'm not cold, no. And I'm not sad," I insisted, "which I don't understand because to top it off, if I'm just the slightest bit careless, I could lose my arm. Looked at from the outside, my life's a failure."

"I don't think so, Colonel."

"What did you say?" I asked, pretending not to have heard her.

"That I don't think you'll lose your arm."

Here was the Andalusian playfulness that I mentioned earlier. I was looking for pity and, respectfully, she was poking fun at me. I thought she did it with grace, and that it was a good sign for my hopes.

There's a shed next to the pond for the keepers of the Retiro, and outside it, on a makeshift grill, one of them was roasting something that from the aroma must have been a chicken. I say from its aroma because the man kept the grill hidden from view, as a security measure in that time of scarcity, but the aroma was unmistakable and I called Magdalena's attention to it.

"Don't worry, Colonel, tonight you officers will have chicken for dinner, too."

All her reassurances had to do with my health or physical well-being, but I contented myself with whatever she said.

The peacefulness of the scene, sunny and cold, was broken by the tramping of a platoon of soldiers on maneuvers taking a shortcut through the park. The man roasting the chicken saw them and picked up the chicken, burning his hands, then disappeared into the shed to keep it completely out of sight from the soldiers, who posed such a risk in that time of scarcity. Magdalena and I laughed with pleasure and complicity. The officer commanding the platoon, as he passed by us, saluted me respectfully, something that didn't always happen in the disorder of those early days of the war, and I noticed that he smiled amiably at Magdalena, who still had a smile on her lips from before. Her white uniform, which I always remember as being so neat and clean, was covered by a heavy blue cloak that set off her blonde hair very handsomely.

She looked very young, but I, too, in the twilight of that Christmas Eve, was young.

~

It was my chest wound that could have cost me my life, but the wound that complicated it the most was the broken elbow, which threatened to make it impossible for me to bend my arm. The doctors at the first hospital advised, and then insisted, that I should be transferred to Barcelona to be put in the care of Dr. Trueta, an orthopedic surgeon with an international reputation.

As best I could, I resisted being transferred from a hospital that had so many positive aspects for me, but common sense and the call of duty prevailed when I was told that the complexity of the fracture could leave my arm immobile. I was already too old to aspire to a younger woman, but especially if I had a physical handicap thrown in. That was the common sense factor. As for the call of duty, I didn't have the right to end up being a noncombatant, in an administrative post, just to satisfy a personal preference.

I don't think I show General Miaja enough consideration in these notes and therefore don't reciprocate the consideration he showed me, although his jokes weren't very on the mark. In this situation, when he found out I had to be transferred to Barcelona, he assigned my own son Antonio as my escort, even though he was too high-ranking to be assigned to escort a colonel. Antonio pretended to be ashamed: "You make me look very bad, Father. I say I don't want to be anywhere near a hero in battle because you heroes are very dangerous, and if you doubt that, look at what happened to my grandfather. But when it comes to traveling and being a tourist, I go as your escort."

I was glad a son of mine could take so much adversity and make a joke out of it.

The one who was happiest about the trip was Sergeant Bermúdez since they provided us with a new car, which he fitted out with an armrest to support my elbow.

I said good-bye to Magdalena, who shook my hand hesitantly and with even more color than usual in her cheeks, which were naturally rosy anyway. Because we weren't alone together, we barely exchanged a word.

Though we were all ready to go, I didn't want to leave Madrid without seeing my brother Ramón, who hadn't been able to visit me in the hospital because his kidneys were giving him a lot of trouble and pain. My younger brothers and I were still minors when my father died, and Ramón became our guardian under the law. To meet the demands of being the head of a big family, he put off his marriage. I say we were a big family because besides the four brothers there were my three sisters, Amelia, Dolores, and Teresa. Ramón married late but very well, to Villaverde's widow. She has a military supply business at number 29 Calle Mayor in Madrid. And I say he married well not only because of the business but also because my sister-in-law is admirable in so many ways. Even though we are now very discouraged about my fate, she keeps fighting for my life and goes to see anybody she thinks might be able to save it. I know she has visited General Varela, the minister of the army, and I'm told he is favorably disposed to me and inclined to pardon my conduct.

So we went to Calle Mayor as part of our preparations

for leaving Madrid, and Ramón was very excited to see me. I found him older and very thin, the latter because of his illness but also because rations were very short, which was no surprise in a city under enemy siege. And especially out of sadness, because his younger brothers, who had been his wards, found themselves in the grip of such a difficult situation, on opposite sides.

Men make plans in vain. If there was any place that a retired colonel of the Civil Guard would be delighted to be, it was at the head of a military supplies business, with the potential not only of selling to the public but also of supplying the security forces and the army, where Ramón had so many friends and such a fine reputation. The sadness of the war, however, and of his own illness, prevented him from enjoying what he had come by late in life, but fairly.

On top of it all, the business had a high turnover, but actual revenues—foreseeably, in wartime—were low. Such revenues as there were barely made ends meet.

It never occurred to us to challenge Ramón about his rank of colonel, but the Ministry of War did challenge it. According to my brother, it miscalculated his years of service and the benefits they entitled him to, retiring him with the rank of lieutenant colonel. He therefore had filed a complaint with the Ministry of Public Administration, which he was always ready to talk about, and that's what we did that day because it was his favorite subject. He was confident that, with the changes that had been made in the ministry, his case would be resolved once and for all. I'm amazed that a man of his lights and aptitude for life should think that in such difficult times somebody would take on an administrative foul-up like that one.

"It's a matter of fairness, Antonio," he would answer, and then go on to show how they had miscalculated his seniority of service.

This visit saddened me. Ramón always advised me in my career like the guardian that he was, and anyway as my older brother, but this time he didn't want to or didn't think it was worthwhile. It seems normal to me now that he didn't, because these were very complicated times and maybe only fools gave advice. The only guidance he gave me, as we said good-bye, was this: "Antonio, take very good care of yourself."

So my departure from Madrid was bittersweet in the end. Sweet on account of the hope I had of returning to the Ritz Hotel and bitter on every other account.

The front had stabilized, but almost inside the city. Many businesses were closed, and there were long lines of people at the food shops. The people were badly dressed, threadbare, and numb with cold, because the cold was especially cruel in that winter of 1937. If I thought driving around among those people in a new car, bundled up and well cared-for, was decadent, how much more so would it have been for me to take refuge in the comfort of a hotel in Paris or Geneva?

At that point the government controlled all the rich parts of Spain: the Mediterranean basin, from Almería to Gerona, and also many major capitals—Madrid, Barcelona, Valencia, Bilbao. . . . I thought, or rather dreamt, that a cease-fire between two evenly balanced forces would be possible. That it wasn't necessary for one of these two Spains to annihilate the other. I say that's what I thought, but as we left Madrid behind and neared the Mediterranean, by Castellón, the bitter cold of the plateau abated and, God forgive me, I went back to thinking about myself. I even forgot about my son José. And above all, the pain in my wounded arm was so intense that I paid more attention to that than to everything around me. How small is man.

Both that Levantine coast and then Catalonia, with their orchards and gardens, vineyards, and farm workers cultivating the land, were a heartening contrast to what I was leaving behind. It's impossible for anybody to live in constant suffering for three years, and I was no exception. I've had to go through a great deal, but there were periods in the war when I thought that was just ordinary life, and I therefore enjoyed everyday things. And even if it's hard to admit it, I've taken part in battles, terrible battles, in which I thought I was doing something useful. That's what I least understand in my current situation. Is there any way to justify our lining ourselves up, facing off against each other, in order inevitably to destroy each other? God can work all sorts of miracles, but I don't believe they will ever include a battle in which men don't die.

And then what I don't understand is that my defense counsel, with the best possible intentions, asked me, "How could you live with the Popular Front of Largo Caballero?" I didn't even know Largo Caballero!

I resign myself to being judged for not having adhered to the rebel Movement that stopped being a rebellion when it came out on top. In any case, I'll be blamed for not knowing that the rebellion was purified by victory. But don't ask me to account for all the things I didn't know, didn't agree to, didn't participate in, just as I don't ask the soldiers sitting in judgment on me in my court-martial how they could fight on the side that committed such terrible repression in Badajoz.

When I leave off recalling my personal memories, my pen is heavy in my hand.

But let me be clear: if I cite the nationalists' repression in Badajoz, it's not because that was the worst in the war but because it was perpetrated by the column commanded by Yagüe, the general to whom it became my duty to surrender the Army of Extremadura. And with me he couldn't have handled himself better. I thought I was going to be facing a butcher, but I found a gentleman who did everything in his power to save my life. How difficult it is to write history, especially when it's so recent. That's why I try to write just my own. And that of the people I love. Those include some who also fought on the other side—José, Alfredo: I was in an agony of fear that they would think they had to participate in the excesses that were being committed on that side.

We professional soldiers were greatly honored by Largo Caballero's government: it abolished the military courts on the theory that we soldiers couldn't be counted on to impose harsh enough sentences, and we were replaced by the so-called People's Tribunals. This was a wrong-headed and doctrinaire thing to do, but at the same time it constituted recognition that we soldiers who were faithful to the constitution weren't useful as instruments of repression. On the other hand, on the nationalist side the military courts' jurisdiction immeasurably increased their authority. That's why it seemed to me that, just as the excesses on our side were the fault of cowardly, acquiescent politicians, the excesses on the other were the doing of my comrades in arms. How much I've suffered over that. The magazines the castle commandant gives me say everything that happened on the winning side was strict justice. If only that were true. To believe it is a vain illusion.

~

My first impression of Barcelona was positive. I was amazed to see a city that, though it was going through a war, didn't look it. I had been bone-cold, and I found myself in the middle of a balmy spring. It was February. People were walking the streets and sitting on the terraces of the rambla with no fear of sirens announcing air raids, and even the workers were dressed as they normally would be, coming and going to work. I did see many anarcho-syndicalists, with their emblems, their belts, and their arms, but it seemed to me there were fewer of them, and they were less obtrusive, than the ones in the war zone I was coming from.

General Aranguren warned me, "Don't kid yourself, Escobar. Things are just where you left them: in the Plaza de Cataluña."

They had promoted my former general to the command of the Catalonia Division, and when I arrived in Barcelona I was one of the first people to congratulate him. General Aranguren had the usual distant air about him that at first gave an impression of aloofness to people who didn't know him well. For example, I didn't understand the comment I just recorded, and when my reaction showed that I didn't, he made a gesture of despair as if it wasn't worth explaining such a complicated subject to a front-line soldier who was good for fighting and not much else. If you could wait, though, he would end up explaining.

"Look, Escobar, what I'm saying is that they're still fighting in the Plaza de Cataluña, using posters now instead of guns. But from words they'll move on to deeds, don't you think?"

Only a fool would treat those words lightly, and I was that fool.

"Maybe not, General."

"Maybe so, Colonel. By the way, when are you going to make general?"

"In the auxiliary services?"

"What do you mean?"

"My left arm bothers me a lot, sir. There are days when I can barely move it."

"And does it hurt you?"

He asked it with all the concern and affection of an old friend. I just nodded. I don't know why, but I didn't usually admit to people that my arm gave me insufferable pain, which could keep me awake all night.

"What a problem pain is," the general said mournfully.

I'm so reluctant to have people feel sorry for me that I went back to the earlier subject. "General, who are the people that are going to go from words to weapons?"

He looked very thoughtful, as though he was going to tell me a secret.

"Listen, Escobar, every self-important jerk's been calling me *tú* for months, and here you are, still calling me

'Your Excellency'. Don't you think it's time you stopped using titles?"

"I wouldn't think of it, General. And now less than ever."

I said it so abruptly that the general was disconcerted. So to prevent him from misinterpreting it, I asked him, "Do you think we're any the less friends because I maintain due respect?"

"Not at all, Escobar, call me whatever you want." He smiled at me agreeably. "What were you asking me before?"

"To tell me who's fighting the battle of the posters in the Plaza de Cataluña before they then move on to using weapons."

"The Communists and the anarchists." The Communists say: "First we have to win the war, and once we've done that we'll have the revolution." And the anarchists answer: "First we'll win the revolution and then the war will have been won, because the war and the revolution are one and the same thing, like light and the sun."

He said it wearily, as being something that was very well known and repeated often in the circles he moved in. But even so he was kind enough to ask me, "What do you think?"

"That we can't give in to either of the two revolutions: not to the soldiers' revolution and not to the anarchists' or Communists'."

"Escobar, do you always believe what you say?"

"I try to. If I didn't, I couldn't go on living."

"It's work to go on living, isn't it?"

"It's harder to die," I answered.

"Well, of course."

He said it with conviction and even enthusiasm. Yet, although they had to execute him sitting in a chair, I have no doubt he was as impressive as ever. And it wouldn't matter, to me, if at that critical moment his distant air made him seem aloof.

~

I also went to pay my compliments to President Companys. I found him very spirited, but thinner and older. I had the impression that everybody was aging except me. I was courting a considerably younger woman, and I couldn't afford the luxury of aging.

Companys had forgotten about my deafness, and I had to make a great effort to follow what he said. Very politely, he spoke to me in Castilian, but he wove in phrases in Catalan. Even though I understand Catalan, it's hard for me to follow if I have to rely on lipreading.

He gave a nice little speech assuring me that Dr. Trueta would fix my arm, and I took it very kindly that he had gone to the trouble of speaking to the doctor personally about my case. The strength of his conviction gave the impression that, if he hadn't gotten involved, even Dr. Trueta's expertise wouldn't have been enough to save my arm. I don't say that as a criticism, and it wouldn't be fitting to criticize a man who is now in as painful a situation as I am. I say it because any show of sympathy was always a great pleasure, especially in those difficult times.

In return, I agreed with everything he went on to say

that I could understand. He explained to me that the terror in our rear guard was in the process of coming to an end. He had succeeded in reclaiming the Palace of Justice from the grip of a revolutionary court famous for the cruelty of its president, the lawyer Samblancat.

"You and I have suffered a lot from excesses like these, remember?" he said.

It wasn't easy to forget, and I felt a bond with him as a friend. We had gone through many troubles together, and even though we were so far apart in our ways of thinking, we were inevitably drawn to each other by what we had suffered and the good things we had been able to do together. I listened to him with pleasure, wanting to believe the many things that had been done to improve the life of the average citizen: primary schools were open again; university life kept going outside the revolution, thanks to the efforts of Professor Bosch Gimpera; life in the city was resuming. . . .

"When they finish fixing your arm you should come live permanently in Barcelona. You have a right to."

He meant that I had earned that privilege by the good work I had done for the city. I thanked him for the invitation and for a moment wondered if Magdalena would like Barcelona. He insisted he would always have a post for me in the Generalitat. Politicians can't always see into the future very clearly. Barely two months after this conversation I would be returning to Barcelona to take up an important post, but quite against Companys' will. We soldiers have no political vision, but we are more practical. Soldiers who get involved in politics are a disaster.

He suddenly asked me, "What do they think in Madrid about the Communists?"

When I didn't answer he went on, "Apparently the Fifth Regiment was outstanding in the battle for Madrid."

To avoid seeming impolite I limited myself to saying, "I can't give an opinion, Mr. President. I was wounded as soon as the attack on Madrid began."

I could have given an opinion, actually, but I didn't want to. Professional soldiers, because we know how to follow orders and fulfill our oath, didn't understand and were very offended by the republican propaganda glorifying the Communist commanders of the Fifth Regiment —Lister, Modesto, El Campesino—which made it seem as though they were the architects of the fight against the uprising.

I don't think Companys was interested in my opinion on the subject but wanted instead to give me his, which was conciliatory toward a Communism that presented itself as moderate, reasonable, and respectful of private property, as opposed to an anarchism that was more intractable every day.

"You've already told me, Escobar, but you realize now that the city belonged to the anarchists that night."

As a matter of fact, the passage of time had confirmed me in exactly the opposite opinion. But I thought it was pointless to argue about it.

Lieutenant Colonel Rojo's opinion reflected a deep suspicion of Communism. He had learned about the terrible purges that Stalin had begun in Russia, but he warned me that many republican politicians wanted to think they were invented by fascist propaganda.

I thought Companys' information would be at least as good as Rojo's, but if I had said so it wouldn't have changed his opinion.

In spite of everything, we were friends. If you can't disagree and still be friends, what sense is there to life?

~

A good proof of our friendship was that when Dr. Trueta saw me he said, "Ah, the famous Colonel Escobar! Companys has told me all about you. He has great sympathy and admiration for you."

Dr. Trueta showed a good deal of interest in my broken arm, so much that it made me nervous. At the time he was the chief surgeon of the Barcelona General Hospital, and although he was young—he would have been about forty—he was very widely known. I don't know what might have become of him.

Like so many men who are really worth something, he spoke to me simply and naturally. He kept me under observation for several days, during which his assistants gave me a lot of attention and at the end of which he gave me his diagnosis in person: "We have to operate on this arm."

I said nothing because he said it so intensely and seriously that I understood the arm had to be amputated. Maybe it was my deafness, or maybe with my lack of medical sophistication I equated an arm operation with an amputation. Or maybe it was because I was so worried that I would be visibly handicapped when I next saw Magdalena. So I begged him, absurdly, "No, Doctor, please! I'd rather live with the pain."

"What's this about? Don't you trust me?"

I didn't know what to say, and he upbraided me: "Where's all your famous courage? You're afraid of a little operation that'll barely take an hour?"

He then went on to explain, in words I could understand, that I had a pinched nerve that would stop being pinched as soon as we put a certain bone back where it belonged.

I was very embarrassed by my mistake, and even when I explained it to the doctor he suspected I wasn't telling the truth and insisted that I would be under anesthetic and it wouldn't hurt at all.

So that was it, and when I had the minor discomfort of the operation and the anesthetic behind me, I was so awed by how well my arm worked and the relief it gave me from the pain that I would have gladly kissed the doctor's hands. For all his intelligence, distracted as he was like everybody in his situation, he always remembered me as the brave colonel who was afraid of a little operation. Examining me after the operation, he said, "What? So you're not afraid any more? See? It wasn't that bad."

It was an exercise in humility for me not to insist on correcting the mistake.

~

I didn't pay my compliments to President Azaña, to avoid seeming presumptuously familiar and out of consideration for his position as head of state. But when he heard about my operation he asked me more than once to come see him, at one point inviting me to dinner at the Palace of Pedralbes.

When we were together just the two of us, after Dr. Trueta had discharged me, an incident occurred that clearly had repercussions and even led to his having an argument with the prime minister, who was still Largo Caballero. That didn't worry me, because everybody knew the two of them had many arguments.

Setting aside normal human deference, I went to see President Azaña to ask him for what I wanted most at that time.

I said that this visit was on the occasion of my having been discharged after my operation. The president of the Republic urged me not to stop taking care of myself and so increase my vulnerability to illness unnecessarily. At one point he volunteered that if there was anything I needed I shouldn't hesitate to ask him. Although he said it just out of courtesy, I set my natural reluctance aside and said, "Thank you, Mr. President, I would in fact like to ask you for a favor."

His expression changed to one of wariness, because we were in a time when he would be asked for favors that would make him very uncomfortable. Maybe he thought I was going to ask for a promotion, or for a posting that wasn't his to give.

"I'd like to go to Lourdes. On a pilgrimage to the Virgin of Lourdes," I said.

He was surprised. "What did you say?"

His surprise bothered me then, but I laugh when I look back on it now.

"I'd like to give thanks to the Virgin for having brought me through this period in good condition. And also to ask our Lady to finish healing this arm."

"Ask what lady?" he said suspiciously.

"The Virgin," I said.

He sat looking at me very intently, disconcerted, and he asked me an amusing question: "Didn't Dr. Trueta do a good job on your arm?"

I said he did, and I showed him so by flexing it.

He continued to be very serious, and without saying anything he rang the bell. When his assistant came in he said, "We need to make arrangements for the colonel to go to France."

The assistant adopted an expression of complicity and mystery, thinking it was about some special mission or other.

"The colonel's going to Lourdes."

"To . . . Lour . . . des?" the assistant stammered in surprise.

"Yes, to Lourdes." The president's tone was intended to make it seem unremarkable.

I listened to the conversation in embarrassment, looking down. When the assistant left, I didn't dare look up. The president, now that he had decided to grant my request, seemed to relax. He got up and went over to the window, with his back to me. This was very characteristic of him.

"I suppose you Catholics are pretty suspicious of me."

He would sometimes turn his back that way in a conversation, not out of rudeness but because he wanted to touch on a delicate subject and was absorbed in thought. That was clear because right after he said that he turned around, looked at me, and said, "I'm not saying that about you particularly, Escobar. Just in general."

Until I had dealings with him I had another image of him. He wasn't very good-looking; he was so unphotogenic that pictures of him put people off. But the sympathetic tone he adopted when he wanted to, and the very precise words he used to express his very lucid thoughts, made you forget all that when you talked with him.

"I'm supposed to have said that Spain's no longer Catholic. And they've seized on that to misinterpret it and misrepresent me as though I were the Antichrist."

I didn't dare make a comment because a Civil Guard knows when he's expected to keep quiet. Besides, I, too, believed he had said what was generally supposed.

"Escobar, I'm not so stupid or unsophisticated as to think that a country stops being religious by an act of parliament. All I meant was that Spain had stopped being clerical. That the institutions of the Church, or at least some of them, had stopped having so much influence on civil life."

I took it as a very great honor that President Azaña should give me such an explanation. Impromptu, I said, "Thank you for your clarification. And I want you to know I think it's good for us Catholics to stop being clerical."

I said this to him because it weighed on me to see how the leaders of the other side often seized on our religion to reduce it to no more than a moral code. I think, God forgive me, that things were clearer on our side: being a Catholic was risky but not required.

"Anyway, Escobar, I'm glad we agree on this, too."

I didn't say anything, but the president saw just from my expression that I had reservations about that agreement, and he added, "I know we don't agree about everything." Then, deep in thought, he said, "Who knows . . ."

~

The government of a nation is a very imposing thing, but in some respects it's similar to a Civil Guard barracks. I mean, in the way disagreements and disputes come to be.

Surprisingly, as I learned later, I had barely crossed the French border with special permission from the president of the Republic before he got a phone call from the prime minister, Largo Caballero, who was alarmed that at such a delicate moment significant military officers would be allowed to leave the country. He was convinced that my pilgrimage to Lourdes was just a pretext for fleeing Spain. And he wasn't the only one; his feeling was shared by a lot of other people. These included even President Azaña himself, who guaranteed Largo Caballero that I would return but at bottom wouldn't have been surprised if I hadn't, given the degree of distaste that he supposed I felt at finding myself in an environment that was so uncongenial to my principles.

I sometimes think I was the only person who thought I was where I belonged.

I made the trip with my son Antonio as my escort and Sergeant Bermúdez at the wheel. Crossing the border, at Puigcerdá, made a very bad impression on me. The border guards seemed to have been shuffled off to simple administrative functions, and the ones who controlled entry and exit were cronies of the local anarchist group.

They didn't treat me with the appropriate respect, which I found especially offensive given that I was carrying the special permission of the president of the Republic. My son Antonio, who is more patient and conciliatory than I am, didn't let me get out of the car and took over the job of processing all the annoying red tape that these men invented, it seemed to me, so they could line their pockets by forging passports and facilitating surreptitious escapes. What a shameful and offensive way to behave, taking advantage of people's vulnerability and fear.

This was my second pilgrimage to Lourdes. I made the first one with my wife when we both knew her illness was incurable, although each of us thought the other didn't know. I went to please her, rather than out of any particular personal devotion. We took a special train for ill pilgrims, and it was there that I began to take consolation from the way my wife showed her exceptional inclination to look after others, in all of whom she found greater need for a cure than in herself. I also took comfort in the fact that she was distracted from her own illness, which was now very severe, especially in the headache pain it involved. My consolation was not great, though, because I couldn't understand why my son José and I had to be left alone when he seemed to need her so much.

My wife followed all the steps prescribed for a good pilgrim, including immersion in the water at the spring, but I don't think she prayed for her life. One morning at dawn, after we prayed the Rosary together at the grotto where the apparitions took place, she said to me very serenely, "If God wants me to die, Antonio, I want to die smiling."

I was seized by such grief that I couldn't hide my tears, which amounted to an admission that her death was certain. Until then we had both pretended it wasn't. A stream runs alongside the grotto in a loud rush, and when I think of that moment I hear the sound of that water still.

That's why I think she went to Lourdes: to ask not for her life but for a good death. And that is what she had.

I bought her a silver medal, the most beautiful one I could find, and she kept it close to her until her death. I have it now. She bought for José an image of the Virgin that was set in a crystal ball. When you gave it a shake, it spread a mantle of artificial snowflakes over our Lady. The boy took the gift as though it were a toy, but ever since his mother left us he has taken the most conscientious care of it. When the problems of politics first emerged with him, I was worried that he had become estranged from religion, but one day, without my having tried to do anything to encourage it, I saw him take the Virgin of the Snows from a hiding place with great care, kneel down before her, and pray.

In life, my wife was very religious and meticulous about practicing her religion, to the point of irritating me, but as she prepared herself to die, she did it with such tenderness and grace that she influenced me, as much as or more than my Franciscan brothers, in the great love I feel for Jesus Christ. In spite of her suffering, the Virgin gave my wife the grace she had asked for on that pilgrimage, and she wore a smile until she lived no longer. How hard it was for me to understand her leaving this life! It's not that I understand it now, but I think God did her a great favor by sparing her all the suffering of this war, which would for her have been extreme, with her sons facing each other on the field of battle and her husband on trial, as a traitor, for his life.

I considered that I owed Our Lady of Lourdes a debt, which was why I asked President Azaña to grant me this favor. I should say, though, that I wasn't going to Lourdes to ask her for a good death as my wife did, but rather to thank her for the blessings I've described and for having more recently saved my life. At the time of my trip I wanted very much to keep on living, and even all the memories I carried with me couldn't make me forget Magdalena. I see no harm of any kind in that, because I've never had an excessively fastidious conscience; and having been so happy in my first marriage, I didn't think it was foolish to try to find happiness again in a second one.

~

My days on that trip were the last calm ones that I had in the war, and maybe in life. My days now, removed as I am from the din of battle, the agitation of politics, the flattering words of the people who esteemed me, the suspicions, the hatreds . . . are also calm. They are calm, but in a shadow of unease cast by I don't know what, although the prosecutor does know: it's cast, he says, by the pangs of a guilty conscience.

Although I asked President Azaña for a week's leave, three days were enough because I lived them with intensity, with a lot of devotion and performing all the acts of piety, not neglecting to immerse my left arm in the fountain so as not to squander the chance to speed up the healing. I did this last surreptitiously, because if Dr.

Trueta had heard about it I think it would have displeased him.

Every day, at dusk, in memory of my previous trip, I would pray the Rosary in front of the grotto with my son Antonio, who came along more to please me than out of devotion. And on the last afternoon of our stay, sitting next to the stream that with the spring rains looked like a river, my son Antonio opened up to me. He told me he had to go back to Spain because that is where his wife and children were. He was just another officer and he didn't have anything to fear. For me, though, things could go very badly. I had nothing to keep me on our side of the war, whereas on the other I had José and Alfredo.

"So do you think I should go over to the other side?" I asked it with the seriousness I assume when I want to tell a joke, although this time I didn't much feel like joking because I saw that even my own son thought I was out of place serving the government. What sadness.

He did look at me warily, knowing my little tricks, but he answered, "No, Father, you can't now. But you could seek asylum in some friendly country. That's what many of the founders of the Republic have done: Ortega y Gasset, Marañón, Menéndez Pidal. . . . They left Spain under a pretext and haven't come back."

I wasn't offended, because a father would have to be a fool to get angry over such well-intentioned advice, even if it was wrong, from a son. I tried to treat it as a teaching moment, as teaching is one of the obligations we have to our children. "They're intellectuals," I said, "and an intellectual can do what he does wherever he may be, but a soldier can be a soldier only in an army."

The countryside surrounding the grotto was very green,

very fresh, with bluish wildflowers and marigolds and daisies of the newly arrived spring. I think of that scene as a contrast to the dry *meseta* that I would be living in after this trip, and the even more rugged terrain on the Extremadura front, deep in drought until the inopportune rains came.

"Your grandfather used to say," I lectured my son, "that war's a horror and, what's more, a useless horror. But if somebody has to make war, we soldiers should make it."

I don't remember having ever heard such a thing from my father, but I invoked him because his grandchildren were very proud of him. There is a monument to my father in Santiago de Cuba. I haven't seen it, but I suppose it would be a collective monument.

"If we win the war," I insisted, "I could be very useful. A lot of things will have to be put right, and order will have to be reestablished."

He tried a weak argument. "And if we lose?"

It was weak because in that spring of 1937 our situation had improved considerably from the point of view of military organization. Nevertheless, I limited myself to saying, "Even then I'll be needed, because when it comes to wars you have to know how to lose them."

I've had to repeat that sentence many times since.

~

This time I did pay my compliments to President Azaña as soon as I got back to Barcelona. I called his assistant on the telephone to let him know I had returned, and the president himself came on the line. He seemed relieved that I was back and cracked some joke about the miraculous waters. It's odd that such an outstanding head of state should be worried about his standing with a prime minister whose days were numbered. That is, with Largo Caballero.

The most intriguing thing is that when I said good-bye to the Catalan authorities this time, to take up my post with the Army of the Center, I did it with the same solemnity as I had the first time. I mean that I bid them farewell as though we were never going to see each other again —not so improbable given the ups and downs of war— and yet I was back in Barcelona again in just a month.

The situation in Madrid couldn't have been more favorable to my plans. The front had stabilized, and the core of the conflict had moved to Vizcaya. I put myself at the disposal of Rojo, who had now been promoted to colonel, and he put me in command of a combat regiment in the University City sector. He confided in me as always and explained, as much as he discreetly could, his most immediate war plans. I particularly noticed one thing about him: his conviction, or his resignation to the fact, that wars take a long time to resolve, so he gave the impression that men could remain in a permanent state of combat readiness. I, on the other hand, dreamt that every one of my actions in the war would foreshadow an end to the conflict by putting the enemy off balance, compelling them to seek an honorable peace. Let me note that, in this respect, I don't regard myself as having had the gift of prophecy.

Colonel Rojo seemed especially cheerful in our conversation, because our forces outnumbered those of the enemy. He concentrated intensely on his strategic and planning tasks, giving the impression that if something wasn't on a map it didn't exist for him. But that was a false impression. With me, at least, he brought up the subjects that I mentioned earlier. We took them up this time so I could tell him about my trip to Lourdes, which gave him great joy, and he made me repeat in detail President Azaña's reaction to my request.

Rojo and I had private subjects of conversation that we would discuss until the end of the war.

I thought the stabilization of the Madrid front was favorable to my plans, which were to court Magdalena, who I supposed wouldn't be sorry to see me again. I'm mortified to think back on it. Not because my hopes were out of place, but because of the store I set by them, focused as I was on my good appearance and how happy she would be when she saw how easily I could move my left arm. These were preoccupations, all of them, more suitable to a cadet than a fiftyish colonel, and even at that I'm understating my age.

Madrid had improved a lot with spring, but the sure signs of war were still there. And hunger hovered over the city, which was the worst situated of all the ones we still had when it came to provisioning it.

I didn't think about any of that when, with the Plaza de Cibeles behind me, protected by sandbags, I turned into the Paseo del Prado, with the magnolias in bloom, and headed for the Ritz Hotel. It was still being used as a military hospital, and it looked better thanks to the orderliness it had taken on by being on a war footing.

I asked at reception for Magdalena the nurse, realizing

as I did it that I didn't know her last name. Another nurse of about my age, whom I also knew but whose name I didn't know, came out to attend me. She greeted me politely, but she took a moment to look me over, as if she didn't recognize me.

"You were asking after Magdalena?"

I nodded, afraid that I had chosen a bad moment for visits, so I excused myself: "I just wanted to say hello to her, but if this isn't the right time I'll come back later."

She thought about it and, after letting out a sigh that would normally have made me feel there was a problem, said, "Come in, come in. We should talk."

She moved with great authority, like a person who was accustomed to command, and I thought she would be the head of the service that Magdalena worked in. I was partly right.

She took me to an out-of-the-way place lined with shelves full of white linen that smelled of disinfectant, a smell that was already familiar to me and was to become even more so. There was no place to sit, so we remained standing.

"Colonel, we know the way you think. Thanks be to God in this case."

This phrase, still in the year 1937, was a very bold thing to say in our zone, but despite it I suspected nothing until this accomplished woman told me straight out.

"Magdalena is a sister. And so am I, naturally."

I have to see the hand of God in all this, because it's inconceivable that, with so many thousand women in all of Spain, my attachment should be to one who would be out of reach for such a reason.

"You'll be able to see Magdalena, of course, but I thought I should inform you about her situation."

Having known so many nuns in my life—my sister, my daughter, Magdalena—this might seem exasperating, or at least it seemed so to my son Antonio. But it has turned out to be a comfort in the critical moment I'm going through now because I realize that there are several religious communities praying for my life, and even though I doubt that their prayers are likely to serve me in this life, I'm sure they will be applied to the next.

The sister's name was and is Anunciación, and to ease my embarrassment over what she had told me, she described how at the beginning of the war all the sisters in her community had been arrested and sent to the Communist secret police, Cheka, in the Circle of Fine Arts, where they thought they were going to die. But one day they were let go. The ones who had family in Madrid went home, and the ones who didn't were sent to work in various hospitals. There were four at the Ritz.

"Do you know who they say saved our lives? La Pasionaria! They say she's saved many sisters. Especially the ones who dedicate themselves to the poor. Could that be true?"

Although I had been left speechless, I managed to answer politely, "In a war anything is possible. What order are you?"

"The Order of Saint John of God."

We had little more to say to each other, but Sister Anunciación, I suppose to keep her conscience clear, said, "Magdalena hasn't yet taken her final vows. She joined the order as an adult. Do you want to see her despite what I've just told you?"

Although I was filled with discouragement and confusion, I think this suggestion pleased me. Or maybe it pleases me now, at a distance. She said it a bit nervously, afraid that I would deflect Magdalena from a vocation that hadn't been confirmed by final vows, not realizing—I think now—that my attraction to her was just a natural one for a man who was suffering and seeking companionship and consolation. It wasn't an unwholesome passion.

"Yes, I'd like to say hello to her."

She was surprised, but she went along with my wish.

We walked along the corridors that had been converted into a wartime hospital. It was orderly, but also sad. All the available space in the foyers, stair landings, dining rooms, and salons was occupied by beds. Magdalena was attending a wounded man in one of them, with a doctor I didn't know. The bed was hidden behind two screens. The patient must have been very seriously wounded. I stood still at a discreet distance but looked intently at her, and when she felt my gaze she raised her head and looked at me. The fact that she was a sister didn't make her any less attractive, in her wonderfully beautiful white uniform. I felt that the last dream of my life was disappearing.

She looked at me, and then she looked at Sister Anunciación and went on with her task. Sister Anunciación went to the bed of the wounded man, spoke to the doctor, and took Magdalena's place. She came toward me. The doctor, still attending the patient, looked at me sidelong, and he maintained that look throughout our conversation. Maybe the whole hospital knew that I was in love with this woman, which would account for his curiosity.

She looked very beautiful, which made me happy. I would like it if all sisters were. My daughter Emilia is.

I'm sure Magdalena smelled of disinfectant, and yet when she came near, her scent cast a spell on me.

I had spent a year—it felt like a century—in barracks, trenches, and hospitals, and the only good thing that had happened to me during that whole bleak time was about to disappear.

We exchanged greetings with a smile, keeping our distance from each other. With the courtesy I'm so proud of because I learned it from my father, I told her about the healing of my arm, and then, with the naturalness that comes from a long life, I raised the subject at hand.

"Your colleague has just told me you're a sister. You don't know how happy that makes me. Did you know I have a daughter who is, too?"

She lowered her gaze and nodded.

Although Sister Anunciación was looking after the wounded patient, she didn't take her eyes off us, and I sensed that she and Magdalena worked together as a team, which didn't seem strange to me because it was a precept in the Corps that Guards went in pairs. Perhaps because of that association of ideas, I said, "When my daughter took her temporary vows, my son Antonio, whom you know, protested because he thought she had a duty to look after her widowed father instead of going into a convent, but I didn't pay any attention to him because I've always thought that being a sister is almost as important as being a Civil Guard."

Magdalena smiled at my comment, and to distract her I added, "But now I've changed my mind: being a sister is more important than being a Civil Guard."

Women are very susceptible to tears, and making jokes to them doesn't change that. So I decided to end the conversation: "Your path's very sure and bright, Magdalena. Mine's very dark."

I didn't know then just how true that was.

"Then may God light it for you, Colonel," she whispered.

"It's the only thing he can do."

I extended my hand to say good-bye to her, and with a trace of coquettishness, she put both of hers behind her back, saying, "It's not customary in our order, Colonel."

Though she couldn't hear us, I think Sister Anunciación understood what we were saying because she came and thanked me when Magdalena returned to her post. Sister Anunciación then extended her hand to say good-bye, which surprised me. I said, "But is it customary in your order to shake hands?"

She smiled as she took my hand in hers.

"It all depends, Colonel, on the circumstances."

I lasted barely a month in that Madrid, so calm, so famished, so austere. At the beginning of May the poppies bloomed in the trenches of University City. I was assigned to a very calm sector, which seemed reasonable to me since I had turned into a very old man. My attraction to Magdalena had taken me back to a youth that disappeared as soon as I gave up the illusion that had sustained it. In the loneliness of my command post I focused on how old I was, and on the possibility—which I had always rejected before—that I should ask for an administrative post as a step toward my retirement.

Uninvolved as I was in politics, I had the impression that the war had stagnated forever. My only job was to make sure the troops in my command suffered as few casualties as possible. This quietest period in the war was also, for me, the most depressing. If I dreamt of peace, I thought the only way to get it was to die of boredom. My depression drove me to think such harebrained things. And if I dreamt of peace, it was to have my son José back again. I hadn't had any news about him or about my brother Alfredo, either one.

In a dizzying turn of events over barely twelve hours, I was informed that the government of the Republic, exercising the powers conferred on it by the Catalan Statute of Autonomy, had decided to take over responsibility for reestablishing public order in Catalonia. This happened on May 4, 1937, I would say at around seven in the evening. To implement the decision, I was appointed general director of public safety of Catalonia. At the same time—I don't know why—General Aranguren was relieved of command of the Fourth Organic Division. All this was communicated to me in person by the marine and air minister, who at the time was Prieto, a socialist. At the same time, he peremptorily ordered me to report at Barcelona as soon as possible.

So my depression lasted just a few days, and I can tell it doesn't come naturally to me because I had hardly received the order before I recovered, if not my youth, at least a youthful drive. Full of energy now, I threw myself very enthusiastically into my assignment, which was the most honorable responsibility they could have entrusted to me because its purpose was to put an end to disorder and anarchy in Barcelona, a city that had won a place in my heart—and that I suppose, despite the zeal of my lawyer, will end up storing me away in its viscera.

I took a twin-engine plane to the airfield at Prat, where Colonel Sandino, the head of the regional air forces, was waiting for me. From there they transferred me—with security precautions that I thought were excessive because I wasn't aware of how serious the situation was—to my old barracks in Calle Ausiàs March. It felt like a leap backward in time: I was back in the barracks of the Civil Guard, where I had been on that July 19, again getting ready to fight against a rebellion that, again, had the Telefónica building as its main focal point—although this time it was occupied by the anarcho-syndicalists, the people who had besieged it earlier.

The officers in my command brought me up-to-date on the situation. The Generalitat's Department of the Interior, headed by Ayguadé, proceeded to bring to an end what had begun on July 20, 1936, and could no longer be tolerated: the CNT's occupation and operation of the Telefónica building. A good move, but long overdue. God forgive me for being vain—which I admit I am, even in my precarious situation—but it would have taken so little on that July 20 for my Guards to reclaim that crucial building, with no greater effort than what we put into taking over the Hotel Colón. The key element was professionalism, and that we always had in plenty. I'm talking about the members of the Corps. But President Companys hesitated for so long that when he did decide to act he provoked another civil war, within the general one. There's no other way to describe what happened that May in Barcelona, although—as seems to be my fate—I was able to experience only the beginnings of it.

Ayguadé and Rodríguez Salas were given the job of taking back the Telefónica building, for which they were counting on a company of Assault Guards, a force that by anyone's lights wasn't strong enough to take decisive action. They therefore had to content themselves with seizing the ground floor, and from there they tried to negotiate with the anarchists who were occupying the rest of the building. It wasn't a negotiation but a war, because in protest against the assault the streets of Barcelona filled with groups of libertarians, young anarchists and their doctrinaire confederates who thought the time had come for the decisive battle of the revolution. That blessed revolution, how much harm it has done us!

I say that on May 5, 1937, Barcelona was a city at war, the way it had been on July 19 of the year before and, interestingly, with similar lines of fire. What hadn't been done then would have to be done now.

One of my first deployments, which I made from my barracks in Ausiàs March, was aimed at calming President Azaña. He was practically under siege by the anarchists in the Palace of Pedralbes, and I had been warned that he—the president of the Republic—was hysterical. He certainly was overwrought, and I had to reprimand him for showing it. But he had reason to be, given the disorder that had gripped the city and the minimal protection he had: sixty soldiers of his presidential battalion armed with rifles, but with no machine guns because the two that he had—he told me on the telephone—he had sent off to the battle of Sigüenza at a desperate moment. He told me this with a touch of bitter humor, adding, "And I haven't been able to get them to give me any more—when everybody and his brother has one here."

So it seemed as though we were engaged in a war fit for an operetta, except that in this one thousands of people died.

I reached out to President Azaña not because of our friendship but because Mr. Prieto, the marine and air minister, had made it my responsibility to take the greatest care of the president's life: it would have been a terrible blot on the Republic, in the eyes of other European nations, for us to lose him in our tragic and shameful internecine battles.

Mr. Tarradellas, the president of the executive council of the Generalitat, helped me enormously in those early stages. I approached him with a certain mistrust, because I considered him responsible for having tried so clumsily and with such inadequate resources to take control of the Telefónica building in which the CNT was now so firmly ensconced.

He very straightforwardly denied that he had approved that effort, which he always openly opposed because it wasn't backed by the resources needed to overcome the resistance it would inevitably meet. He said the president of the Republic would vouch for what he said, but he didn't have to provide any proof, not only because it would have served no purpose but also because he spoke so convincingly. It was too bad that President Companys hadn't paid more attention to him because Tarradellas is, or was, a man of great common sense who fought doggedly from March 1937 on to unify all the Catalan police in a single force, thereby dissolving the patrols of control, which were in fact controlled by the CNT and were committing such outrages. What's more, Tarradellas reached the point of forbidding members of the police to have any political affiliation at all, a supremely wise measure that to a Civil Guard would have been elementary. But his fellow members of the council didn't see it that way, so we found ourselves plunged into another civil war months later.

He gave me all the information he could to help me with my mission, including information about the state of mind of the president of the Generalitat, who saw the central government as having dispossessed him of his authority in matters of public order. Tarradellas told me, very candidly, that when Companys heard about my appointment to this post he said, "This is the least of many evils." I took this as a compliment. It seems, too, according to what I learned later, that President Companys also said you should never underestimate the Civil Guard, and that I had told him they would someday have to call on me to restore order. I think I did say that, in a moment of vehemence and irritation on that July 19, 1936. Things turned out that way, not in fulfillment of a prophecy but as a fluke of fortune, or because it was the will of Providence that death should always hover over me.

I don't think they were all that unhappy in the Generalitat to be relieved of what was at the time such an exasperating responsibility.

As usual, I tried to move quickly to do what had to be done. In my telephone conversation with President Azaña, he told me Mr. Prieto had put two destroyers at his disposal, as well as the air forces commanded by Colonel Sandino. But he said it with the bitterness that so undermined his effectiveness, warning me that he regarded the offers as a *mere courtesy*. I didn't see it that way, and as soon as I determined that the destroyers had anchored in the harbor of Barcelona—which happened in the early hours of May 5—I got in touch with their commanders, invoking my own authority supplemented as necessary by that of the president of the Republic. The destroyers were the *Lepanto* and the *Sánchez-Barcáiztegui*, each of them with a complement of marines.

I was in nonstop meetings at the barracks in Calle Ausiàs March, attended by a junta made up of people whose names I don't remember because, in their indecision and fear, they were of very little help to me.

But the anarchists, too, had formed a junta—a revolutionary one, in their case. It announced categorically that everybody responsible for the attack on the Telefónica building would be shot.

When I informed the members of my junta that the destroyers I've mentioned were anchored in the city's harbor, a political commissar, voicing the cowardice of the others, warned me, "I believe that using the forces of the navy could be a provocation to the Catalan people. And they're not necessary to suppress a rebellion."

"This isn't a rebellion," I answered. "It's a civil war within another civil war. I'll use all the forces the government makes available to me to end it as soon as possible. If the minister, Mr. Prieto, has sent two destroyers, I'll make full use of them."

"And I'm telling you that the Catalan people won't tolerate it," the man said angrily.

"The Catalan people are no different from the other peoples of Spain, who want only one thing: peace." (How convinced I was of this!)

"I advise the marines not to show themselves in public."

He was shouting now, and it seemed like more of an order than advice. I therefore answered, very calmly, "Your advice has come too late. The marines are already marching through the streets."

This was true. The marines marched down the dockside, in correct formation and correctly uniformed. That was what I had ordered the commanders of the ships to send them out to do. The navy, though it hasn't attained the precision of the Civil Guard, has always marched very well. I thought it was important for them to do it for the same reasons that I required it of my Guards on July 19. We were right. The merchants who had shuttered their shops, the neighbors hidden in their houses, the women, the children, the employees, came to their windows and filled the sidewalks to cheer the marines. The people had endured many months of being subjected to the whims of the patrols of control.

For the same reason and with the agreement of Colonel Sandino, twenty planes of the third air region, plus the air forces of the airfield at Reus, began a series of threatening flights at low altitude over the city.

I think the anarchists understood we weren't going to argue with them on the street corners any more.

~

"You don't have much of an instinct for conservation," Colonel Rojo once said to me.

With my deafness, I misunderstood the word and thought fault was being found with my *conversation*, so although I was surprised I begged his pardon for my lack of sociability. What a silly misunderstanding! We laughed a lot when we had sorted it out, though that didn't put an end to my amusement at having been thought of as reckless.

My father risked his life so many times that it seemed he too lacked an instinct for conservation, but actually what was happening was that he had such a highly developed instinct for helping his family rise in the world, without compromising his honor or his country, that he didn't have much choice but to risk his life.

I love life, and I've never risked my own without good and sufficient reason.

I still love it, even now, although there may not be much of it left to conserve. I love this little rough pine table I'm writing on. I pay great attention to keeping it clean, scrubbing it carefully with a wire brush to remove grease and ink stains. I'm grateful for the cot in my cell, which because it's very hard, makes it possible for me to sleep in peace. I'm grateful for every ray of sunshine that comes through the bars on my skylight, the blue sky, the white clouds, and the darkness that keeps me company at night. But above all I'm grateful for these sheets of paper, which are sometimes wrinkled, always yellowed, of which I now have about a hundred covered with my handwriting in purple ink. They convince me that, although I may be just an average soldier, I'm an excellent penman.

This reassurance, and even defense, is relevant because the steps I took as I've just described produced a truce in the street fighting, which I thought was a good omen. So I called President Azaña to let him know. At the same time I informed him that I was headed to the Ministry of Governance, the better to direct the ongoing operations. The president urged me very strongly not to do that and instead to stay in barracks, because the streets were still very dangerous.

I didn't think the streets were dangerous enough to justify compromising the discharge of my responsibilities, and I thought this not on a whim but for a reason: as the director of public order I needed all the backing and the support resources of the ministry.

We took appropriate precautions for my transfer there. I sat in the back seat of my car, with a Guard on either side of me, another one in the front seat, and Sergeant Bermúdez at the wheel. I had an escort of two vehicles, each of which carried, besides the Guards who were sitting inside, four more Guards standing on the mudguards so they could get a clearer view of the places we had to pass through, although the distance to the ministry wasn't great.

My guards were all from the Civil Guard, assigned

at the time to the National Republican Guard. Despite my confidence in such company, I wasn't unconcerned. Quite the contrary, which is clear from the fact that, as we neared the ministry, I was the first to see and to warn that two mattresses, on the terrace of a two-story building, were being pushed apart to reveal a machine gun on its tripod. Even before I saw it I shouted to Sergeant Bermúdez, "Step on it!"

These were the only words I got out because I leaned forward as I said them, and at that moment the machine gun, very precisely aimed at me, raked me with seven bullets. I didn't feel any pain at all—just a great dizziness, aggravated by the swerves that Sergeant Bermúdez began to execute to make us a harder target for the attackers. With so many holes in me, of course, I was bleeding heavily and suddenly lost consciousness.

I was the only one wounded. None of the Guards accompanying me were even grazed. I mean, in the attack. I don't know what happened in the escorting vehicles when they fought back.

It was an assassination attempt—as became clear later—and not a case of general street violence. I don't say that as a defense to what people said afterward about what I had done: that it was my pride that exposed me to attack because I hadn't wanted to negotiate with the anarchists when I assumed my post as director of public order in Catalonia. The supporting argument they make is that my successors in that role did negotiate and they were never subjected to such an attack.

The reason I didn't negotiate is that I didn't receive any instructions or authorization to do so. And if my successors could negotiate in the aftermath, I think it was because what I had done convinced the anarchists that they didn't have much chance of getting their way.

I should mention that the political commissar—the spokesman for the junta that was assisting me in the Ausiàs March barracks—demanded, "Aren't you thinking of consulting Comrade Federica?" That's what they called Montseny, whom I didn't get to know personally. She was a woman with ideals, so convinced the revolution was necessary that she thought all of us were of the same opinion.

I didn't think of consulting her, even for a moment, and I'm confident that God wouldn't attribute that to personal pride but rather to the importance of what I stood for at the time, in my position as the head of public order in this part of the world that I so love.

I regret so many of my past actions that, if I were a good penitent, I would have to bore my confessor stiff describing them all. But I didn't regret that one. As time goes by and I look back on it now, my decision on a day that did so much to end the revolution consoles me in my many disappointments.

~

I never had a better opportunity after that to die in the line of duty. When they admitted me to the hospital they thought I would seize that opportunity, because I had hardly any blood left in my veins. They thought one of the bullets had cut through my spine, and there was no cure for that. I was declared clinically dead, as I had been on the other occasion. But you can see that what the doctors say isn't dispositive, because if God disposes otherwise, you keep on living. I find this firmness of purpose on the part of the Creator, regarding my case, unfathomable.

I won't tell the story of how I got well again, because it would just be repeating the story of the last time, except that the nurse who took care of me had an abrupt manner and was very slovenly, and so unattractive that being a widower didn't seem like such a bad thing.

I remembered Magdalena, and I still go on remembering her.

I don't remember how many operations they performed on me. The bullet that affected my spine didn't cut it through, as they had thought at first. It was grazed, leaving me slightly paraplegic and requiring me to sleep on a wooden plank. That's why the cot in my cell seems to serve me well.

They allowed visitors at the end of May, and President Azaña was among the first. It was one of the few times that I remember seeing him pleased and hopeful. As though to downplay the honor that his visit to me represented, he said, "Don't worry, Escobar, it's good for me to escape from my pen once in a while. You look very good, although you're thinner."

I excused myself by saying, "Well, I'm thinner because it seems that my wounds made me lose a lot of blood."

The president laughed because it was ridiculous for me to excuse myself, but at the same time, referring to his quite prominent paunch, he said, "Ah, that would be a good thing for some of us politicians, but of course politicians attack each other with words, and they don't kill. They don't draw blood, either."

It was a sarcastic comment, but he didn't say it with his usual bitterness. He was that content, he explained to me, that we were done with the revolution within the Republic.

"How can we accuse the military of rebellion," he said, "if we ourselves tolerate a revolution in our own breast?"

Then, reflectively, as though he had thought hard about it, he added, "All the mistakes we make while we're maintaining the legal government against the rebels are their responsibility."

He was full of praise for what I had done in those first moments, although he too found fault with me for recklessness. I barely had the strength to defend myself. And it wouldn't have been polite because, to show me how highly I was esteemed, he said that my being wounded would require dividing my job in two because they wouldn't be able to find anybody who was up to doing the whole of it. I think he was exaggerating.

The seemingly impossible happened again. I was healed, at least enough to be discharged from the hospital and go back into service. I had to walk with a cane, but I tried to hold myself very erect, so as not to lose the military bearing that I'm afraid has become a point of vanity with me.

In the full bloom of spring, the city couldn't have been more beautiful, which made it a great source of satisfaction for me to walk its now orderly streets, without seeing uniforms that weren't regulation. But I was posted again to the Army of the Center, and I had to go back to it once more.

I exercised restraint in saying my good-byes to the many friends I had here, thinking that if I made too much of them I would be back immediately. It's true that I've returned, but I'm not in a position to say hello to anybody.

In Madrid they assigned me to the Brunete sector, where I was unexpectedly promoted. What began as a surprise attack by our army, to lift the nationalist siege that had us tied down in the western part of the capital, turned into a colossal battle when Franco's proud and fiercely unyielding troops, who never willingly gave the least little bit of ground, launched a counteroffensive. The bloodiest part of the battle coincided with the suffocating heat of July. Even the officers, including the field-grade officers, were thirsty.

We advanced far enough to recover the villages of Quijorna, Villanueva de la Cañada, and Villanueva del Pardillo. That was reason enough to count this battle as a great triumph for the Republic. But its value shouldn't be exaggerated: the small gain in territory cost us many lives, and we gave the enemy the chance to use the Messerschmitt fighters of the Germans' Condor Legion for the first time. They concerned me a good deal because as far as I could tell they were so much better than the Russian-made "Chatos" that went up against them.

This impulse to glorify the victory came from Dr. Negrín, the new prime minister and successor to Largo Caballero, who after the May Days in Barcelona had to resign.

Negrín's appointment was well-received because he came from an upstanding family and he himself showed signs of being upstanding in the first months of the war, helping to rescue many people from the revolutionary Cheka. A very cultivated physician, he was professor of physiology at the University of Madrid. As finance minister he had very efficiently reorganized the border guards, which marked him as a man of common sense. These border guards were the ones who enabled us to recover all the posts on the border with France, which as I've said, had been under the anarchists' control.

I had had no relationship with Largo Caballero, but I dealt personally with Dr. Negrín and even had to stand up to him as the war was coming to its end. He was very sure of his talents, of which he had many, and he thought he could bend the Communists to his will as he pleased. A serious mistake.

Rereading these pages, I worry that I get too angry with the anarchists and thereby feed the legend that those unfortunate people were natural enemies of the Civil Guard, as if it were natural for our Corps to have any enemies. They put me through a lot of suffering, and I've just finished describing how they wanted to end my life in Barcelona, but I nevertheless had friends among them; and when we suppressed the people's militias the men joined the army and successfully became brave, long-suffering soldiers. I also had friends among the Communists, but their friendship was limited by the instructions they were getting from the party. Unfortunately, that was easy to see in some of my officers in the Army of Extremadura.

While I'm making comparisons, I think a man like Melchor Rodríguez, the selfless director of prisons, whom I so admire for how he risked his life to save the lives of others, could handle the anarchists but not the Communists. The latter were treated with great respect by the leaders of the Republic, however, who saw in them a protection as much against the anarchist revolution as against the fascist one. When the danger of the first disappeared, from the spring of 1937 on, Dr. Negrín sought the help of the Communists in putting an end to the second.

I'm clearly being critical of Prime Minister Negrín, and yet it was he who promoted me to general, a thing that I never thought would come to pass because the criteria for promoting professional soldiers were very high.

~

I don't know what my reaction was to this promotion. A soldier is naturally disposed in favor of his advancement, and I don't think I was any exception. I understood that my promotion meant that all my father's efforts to foster flourishing military careers for us had borne fruit. But it was hard to take complete satisfaction in it in such a shattering situation. And, during those months, I was feeling especially shattered.

One October day in that year 1937, I was sitting in my army tent in front of Quijorna, enjoying the calm of a Castilian fall, which if September has been rainy, makes its appearance in October as a burst of spring greenery.

The calm of the season complemented a lull in the war in my sector, because the core of the fighting had moved to the Aragon offensive.

I wasn't outside the tent enjoying the day's beautiful

weather but inside, doing the exercises that had been prescribed to ease the discomfort in my spinal column.

Because I had my back to the tent's entrance I didn't see Sergeant Bermúdez's face when he announced the visit of my daughter-in-law Angelita, Antonio's wife, and I thoughtlessly had a rush of great happiness because I like her so much. I asked the sergeant to help me put on my tunic because although she was a member of the family, I didn't like receiving a lady in shirtsleeves. As I was buttoning it up, it occurred to me that it was unusual for a woman to come to the front, no matter how calm it was. She came into the tent and I kissed her on the cheeks, which I noticed were damp, with that salty dampness that leaves little room for doubt as to its origin.

"What's happening, Angelita? Has something happened to Antonio?"

She shook her head as the tears poured out, with no attempt now to hide them.

"But where's Antonio?"

"In Belchite."

This little village in Aragon was much discussed in those days because our government had launched an intense effort to take it and the nationalists had made an equally intense effort to hold it.

Angelita is not a woman to cry without a very good reason, and if nothing had happened to Antonio, there were very few alternative reasons for so many tears.

"What is it?" I asked her, grimly resigned.

I remember that Sergeant Bermúdez, against all habit and discipline, hadn't moved from the spot where he was standing when he let Angelita pass.

"José—" Angelita said to me, her voice breaking.

This word did me more damage than all the bullets I had taken put together.

I realized that Sergeant Bermúdez was also streaming tears, and yet I asked, "Are you sure he died?"

"Yes, Father, he was in Belchite with the Falangists who were defending it. Some prisoners told Antonio when they took Belchite."

I don't know where he's buried. And, now, I have no right to any information about him. I've been told only that he died, together with other Falangists and Carlists, putting up a heroic defense of Belchite, which he hadn't even had the chance to get to know.

We love all our children equally, but José was left so alone when his mother died that it seemed to me I had to compensate by devoting all my free time to him. The boy waited excitedly for Sunday, so he could go out with me. He would have been fourteen then, and still in short pants. If I had to work on a holiday, I would take him to barracks, and even when he was bored he didn't complain because he was near me.

I would do for his sake what I never would have done otherwise. We would go to the children's showing at the movies on Sundays to see Tom Mix, who was his favorite until he fell in love with Shirley Temple. He enjoyed himself so much at the movies that it was worth it to me just to see him having a good time.

He was always so polite and considerate with me that, if he could, I'm sure he would beg my pardon for the very great sadness I feel over his death. Even now my tears blot these pages.

But on that October day I was unable to cry. I sat down in a chair as Angelita and Sergeant Bermúdez did the same. I sat down because I couldn't stand.

~

When my wife died, she left behind for me our everyday life: chairs, armchairs, tables, beds, clothes—permanent reminders that were there for me to see even though she wasn't. The pain was spread out over many long days. José's death left a sudden, total void, with only distant memories because I hadn't seen him for a long time. Without the consolation of keeping vigil over his body, or the sorrow of burying him.

I felt as though my days on earth had already come to an end.

I also began to wonder whether I myself was the one who had led him to his death, by my determination to pull him out of what seemed like an outbreak of rebellion that July 19. Fortunately, I don't have a perfectionist conscience. I did what any father would have done in my place. If it wasn't for the best, it was because I didn't know any better.

Antonio came back from Belchite overwhelmed by the bitterness of having faced his brother across the trenches. That's why I say this war has been particularly fratricidal for the Escobar family. Yet I'm afraid our case hasn't been exceptional.

I spent the winter of 1938 with this void in my heart, with my days on earth at an end but fulfilling my obligations nevertheless, and I even found relief in doing so. I participated in the campaign of the Levant.

The sadness of losing my son went hand in hand with the fact that the war was so senseless. If it was always so for me, it was even more so when two regular armies went head to head—both of them led by professional soldiers, though there was more evidence of that on our side than on the other, because the field officers we drew from the militias were very few and mostly had lesser commands. One I do remember was Cipriano Mera, a very honorable anarchist who rose to command an army corps with the rank of lieutenant colonel. And there were three full colonels who were very well known to be members of the Communist Party—Lister, Modesto, and Tagüeña—who rose to divisional command. So did El Campesino, but I prefer not to talk about him.

I say ours was a regular army, with the discipline of being in uniform. After my promotion to general I was addressed as Your Excellency, as has always been the custom in the militia, without my having to require it. Things unfortunately weren't the same on the other side, and it came as a painful surprise to see a picture of General Franco wearing a black coat, blue shirt, and red beret, raising his arm in salute in the style of the Italian and German fascists. I didn't understand how such a highly regarded soldier could allow himself to be shown that way. Dr. Negrín took care to publish graphic evidence like this photo, so there would be no doubt about the growing politicization of the nationalists.

My son José gave his life for what that blue shirt represented, and that was reason enough for me to respect it, but I didn't think the general-in-chief of the opposing army needed to wear it. Seeing him in it made it hard to believe we weren't fighting against fascism. I freely vented my feelings on the subject to General Rojo. He had been promoted to general several months after I was, and we had occasion that year to have many dealings with each other in the line of duty, but we always reserved some time for exchanging personal impressions. He provided me with information, of which he had a great deal as chief of the general staff. He was the one who told me how the Vatican was alarmed by General Franco's sudden Falangist fervor, seeing it as boding a possible European war between fascism and the democracies. How complicated, Lord, is life!

~

I had occasion to experience that complexity when in October 1938 I was summoned to the headquarters of General Miaja, who was now captain general. I was depressed for so many reasons, and the only place I found relief was in performing my duties, not because I was dedicated but because of the diversion it involved and the chance to be of help to people who needed it. I did some work with the libertarian Melchor Rodríguez, the director of prisons, who accused the Communists very assertively of having their own jails with interrogation rooms. I think it was true, but we didn't have much success because we didn't get any support from Prime Minister Negrín. He always firmly denied that the Communist Cheka operated in Spain. Only he would know why.

Speaking of this subject, I remember that President Azaña, when he called me in to see him in Valencia during the campaign in the Levant so he could congratulate me on my promotion to general, confided in me how much he had insisted to Dr. Negrín that I be named the Republic's director general of security. The prime minister put it off, arguing that the merger of the Civil Guard with the Assault Guards had produced dissatisfaction in the ranks of the latter, and that given my background in the Civil Guard, my appointment could be a new bone of contention.

I thanked President Azaña for his good wishes. That post would have given me a chance to do many useful things, and I think I was right for it given my experience in matters of public order. But, as I say, I was summoned by General Miaja to take command of the Army of Extremadura, as general-in-chief, while I was laboring through life in such low spirits during that fall of 1938.

I resisted the commission because I considered it beyond my abilities. The Republic was fielding four armies during that period: the Army of Catalonia and the Levant, which General Hernández Saravia commanded; the Army of Andalusia, commanded by the Marquess of Oroquieta, whose family name was Moriones; the Army of the Center, under the command of General Miaja himself, soon to be replaced by Colonel Casado; and the Army of Extremadura, which I was being ordered to command. It was hard for me to believe that among our whole array of illustrious soldiers there wouldn't be another one more qualified than I was for such an important commission. So I went to see General Rojo; it was very clear that all appointments originated with him, even though General Miaja made them.

As he did in all my conversations with him, he called me General throughout this one, a courtesy that I learned to accept with good-natured irony because it came from a man who, when he was just a lieutenant colonel, already commanded more than all the generals put together. As a pretext for using this form of address, he cited the fact that my promotion to general antedated his.

Not out of modesty but because of my low spirits, I reminded him that I started out as a buck sergeant. As though he had already settled the subject in his mind, he interrupted me: "So you've had a better career than I have. Remember that now you're general-in-chief of the Army of Extremadura, with three army corps under your command, consisting of eight divisions. What do you think of that?"

"That it's too much for a buck sergeant."

"Don't you believe it. When you act, the virtues of the old buck sergeant will be reborn in you, and they're what we need right now."

As though he had spent too much time in digressions, and with the dispatch that was so characteristic of him, he got up, took up the pointer, and went to the wall map of operations. He explained Plan P to me, consisting of a combined operation between the fleet and the Army of Extremadura, aimed at reestablishing the front in the middle of the peninsula. Admiral Buiza, in command of the fleet, would attack Motril, debarking a special brigade that could march on Málaga with the goal of forcing Queipo de Llano's army to divert forces to the coast. When Rojo got to this point, he looked intently at me and said urgently, "This would allow your army to break the front in the Sierra Trapera and open the way for your forces into Andalusia."

The force of Rojo's conviction was so great that I found myself agreeing to a plan which, if it worked, would divide the peninsula in two.

"If we pull it off, Franco will have to take troops away from the advance on Catalonia. That would mean the reestablishment of balance between our forces."

Because I was looking doubtful, he insisted, "No, General, don't be skeptical. Franco never accepts the loss of even a sliver of territory. He does what he has to do to get it back."

When he put away the pointer and sat down at his table, I let the cup of my bitterness run over in spite of my confidence in him: "And then what? Is this war never going to end?"

Just as Rojo was very human when it came to personal problems—he offered profound condolences when he learned of José's death—he was very cold when it came to strategy.

"My only obligation is to produce a balanced military situation that will enable our politicians to negotiate peace with Franco."

A sad mission, to undertake such a bloody campaign in order to make peace possible. Despite it all, I accepted. To be cheerful, General Rojo joked, "If this works out well, it'll go down in history."

"And who will history remember—you or me?"

"You, of course, because you'll be in command of the troops."

"Ah, look out! President Azaña warned me against that. Going down in history's very dangerous."

General Rojo's eyes sparkled happily through his round, old-fashioned lenses. It was very important, in those difficult days, to have a friend you could joke with.

~

I assumed my new post on October 23, 1938, in a hurry because I had been told that Plan Motril would have to be carried out in the fall. And so it should have been, but —I don't know why—it was delayed for too long.

The Army of Extremadura was known for being disorganized, for the confusion that prevailed among its mid-level officers, and for the prevalence of Communist officers. I worked hard to remedy all this as much as I could. This lifted my spirits, because it pleased me very much to have an army in good order.

And speaking of order, it seemed to me particularly important to attend to the spiritual needs of the Catholics who fought in my army. There were quite a few of them, especially in the corps commanded by Colonel Ibarrola, which was made up of many of his fellow Basques. Like me, Ibarrola came from the Civil Guard.

I went ahead with my plan to meet these spiritual needs on the basis of the fact that Prime Minister Negrín had recently authorized private religious services in Catalonia.

I saw no reason why such an important need on our part would have a lower priority than the Catalans' needs.

Finding a place to hold the Masses was easier than finding a priest to hold them, because the priests who were in hiding in the area distrusted us deeply. They had every reason to be wary, given the brutal persecution they had suffered at the beginning of the war. It was my captain adjutant, Pedro Masips, a very effective and useful man in every way, who learned that a priest was hiding in the village of El Viso and promptly brought him to my headquarters at Almadén. Either Masips didn't give him too many explanations or the ones he did give weren't very convincing, but in any case the man didn't begin to relax until I kissed his hand. And even then he couldn't believe we were going to celebrate Mass every day, which is what I had firmly in mind. It took time, but he did come to believe it. From November 5, 1938, on, in the Army of Extremadura, Mass was celebrated in the field every day, and I remember with particular emotion the Mass held on December 24, which we celebrated at midnight as the liturgy prescribes. There was such a big turnout that, even though the space was big enough to accommodate a good many people, some of them had to stand outside. Civilians from Almadén also attended.

The moon was full, I remember, and it was very peaceful and serene. Although it was a private Mass, a committee was formed to preside over it, which I chaired with Colonel Ibarrola at my right, along with other officers from field grade on down. We wore parade dress instead of our campaign uniforms. I missed wearing my dress uniform, which I wore when I was a commander in the

Civil Guard, for the occasion. We built a very handsome altar, lit by twelve candles set in beautiful candelabra. Two other priests who had become a part of my army officiated with Father Julián, which was the name of the priest from El Viso. We duly sang, in Latin, "Gloria in excelsis Deo et in terra pax hominibus bonae voluntatis", and more than just one of us had to fight back tears. There was every reason for that. While we prayed to the Lord for peace on earth for men of good will, we were at the ready from day to day waiting for the order to launch the offensive of Extremadura. The order finally came on January 5, 1939, the eve of Epiphany.

~

Under the command of Colonel Ibarrola, the Twenty-Second Army Corps got our attack off before dawn to a very forceful and successful start. By eight in the morning we had succeeded in breaching the nationalist line in the Sierra Trapera.

We occupied the peak of Patuda and the Montenegro escarpment, opening a breach over four miles wide and clearing the way for the bulk of our army to advance. Our drive on that first day was very productive, and we were able to cross the river Zújar near its source.

The cost in human lives was high, mostly because of harrassment by enemy planes, their machine guns raking us as they flew low overhead.

The following day, January 6, with the support of the two divisions making up the Toral Group, the Twenty-

Second Army Corps had achieved penetration of almost twenty-five miles, enabling us to take Fuenteovejuna and Granja de Torrehermosa on January 7.

I knew that our possession of these points would further our advance toward Cordoba and Seville, which if successful would have been a decisive step forward in carrying out our plans. But before attempting that we had to neutralize the threat from the terrain adjoining our flanks, which was still in the hands of the nationalists, to prevent them from encircling my army and trapping it in a pocket. I strongly insisted on this and can't complain about the help I got on it, because Miaja, who was at the time the commander-in-chief of the whole Republican Army, sent me five divisions as reinforcements. This was no surprise. General Rojo made it very plain that this battle would clarify the final phase of the war, and so right he was.

The land offensive that had developed so favorably didn't have its counterpart at sea: the planned debarkation at Motril of Admiral Buiza's fleet didn't come to pass. What did come to pass, unexpectedly, was the end of a long drought: torrents of cold rain and sometimes sleet, along with snow in the heights of the Sierra. The rain and snow were so intense that our heavy equipment couldn't move. The waters of the Zújar overflowed their banks, flooding the adjoining terrain and submerging our trucks. I myself had to cover the front on horseback because motorized transport quickly became impossible. The drought had lasted so long and the roads were so dusty that the first rains turned them into bogs, and the rains that followed into great sheets of standing water.

These conditions forced me to call a halt to our advance to await better weather and the longed-for disembarkation in Motril that would have helped us so much.

I suffered a great deal to see my soldiers barely half-equipped for so much cold and wet.

~

The moral pain I felt at seeing such misery in others was in addition to my own physical suffering, caused by my spinal paraplegia, which was greatly aggravated by the wetness and having to get around on horseback. I had trouble sleeping at night. One night, as I was trying to do so, my captain adjutant asked for my signature on a document that was so short I thought it was just routine red tape.

It was a death sentence for a soldier in the Toral Group who had been accused of desertion in the face of the enemy. The sentence required the signature of the general-in-chief of the army—my signature—because it was the maximum sentence. And since it was to be carried out that very night, before dawn, the signature was required at this inconvenient time.

I couldn't understand how we could take a man's life with such a short document, so badly scrawled, so I asked my captain adjutant to get me the Code of Military Justice. I was no expert, but when I read it and put the sentence up against it, I could see how slapdash the latter was.

Despite the bad timing—it was one in the morning—I wanted to see the presumed deserter. I will never forget his terrified face when I ordered the door to his cell to be opened, because he thought we were the ones who would be executing him.

"Why didn't you want to cross the river on the ninth?"

The soldier was struck dumb with fear and couldn't answer me. Captain Masips, who was with me, tried to calm him down.

"Answer His Excellency. The general wants to help you."

Under the circumstances, and with so little light, the condemned man didn't even know who was talking to him. He decided, with Captain Masips insisting, to answer anyway.

"I'm sick."

You could see that from the trembling of his body, which couldn't be wholly attributed to his fear of what was in store for him.

"And on the ninth, were you sick then, too?"

"Yes, General, my chest hurts and I'm always cold."

He was a young boy, with close-cropped hair and an emaciated face. He was nineteen. I touched his forehead, which was burning hot. I vented my anger on the jailer, who was a sergeant. I don't know why. Maybe because he couldn't be bothered to ease the last hours of a man's life and left him stretched out there, in a damp barracks, with an old blanket that was barely big enough to cover him. Maybe I got angry because my back was hurting a lot. What I do know is that we went to find first the judge advocate captain and then the major who had presided at the court-martial. I don't remember the name of the major, and anyway I don't think that's relevant.

The major was sleeping still in his clothes, not having had the chance to undress in those intense days of the war. He had come from the militias and wasn't very used to hierarchies. When he understood the reason for my visit, he dared to say to me, "And you woke me up at this hour for one private?"

"Even if he's just a private, he can't be that without being a man, and there's a Code of Military Justice that this sentence violates in three ways out of four!"

"General, we can't operate in this war with a lot of technicalities!"

"We can when a man's life depends on it!"

"But how can you talk to me about the life of one man when all around me hundreds are dying every day?"

"I can't avoid those deaths, but this one I can!"

The major saw how determined I was, and his anger died down.

"All right, General, what do you want me to do?"

"Hold a new court-martial."

The major stood thinking, and I added, "Now."

"At three in the morning?" He became indignant again, and because he wasn't stupid he asked the judge advocate captain, "Does he have the right to make me do that?"

The latter, who was also against it because of the inconvenience I was creating for them at this unholy hour, turned to me with seeming respect. "Your Excellency has the right not to sign the sentence, in which case the trial record will go up for review in the fourth chamber of the Supreme Court."

In the light of which I addressed myself humbly to the major: "Major, may I ask you as a favor to convene this court-martial? A nineteen-year-old boy is expecting to be shot at dawn."

The man agreed. "Yes, General."

"Thank you very much."

As I finish writing this, remembering the kindness of that soldier, his name comes back to me: he was Major Benigno Castedo, of the Toral Group.

The young private's name was José García Bardiel, and his life was saved. At least, from being executed by firing squad. They admitted him to the hospital because he was suffering from acute pneumonia.

~

The debarkation of the fleet at Motril never took place, and nobody could explain to me why. Colonel Ibarrola, who strove so hard at the head of his army corps to attain the objectives he had been assigned, almost cried when this desertion was confirmed to him.

But we had exhausted our capacity for tears, having shed them for so many men who had left their lives in these mountains and plains.

The High Command congratulated us on the penetration we had achieved.

~

On February 25 I got a confidential communication from the prime minister Dr. Negrín summoning me to the airfield at Los Llanos, Albacete. He asked me to travel with a low profile. Since Albacete was in our rear guard, I did without an escort and was accompanied only by Captain Masips and our driver Sergeant Bermúdez, whose years of service would have earned him a promotion to lieutenant by now.

I didn't know the reason for the trip, although I supposed it was important given the personal invitation from the prime minister.

We were taken from the airfield to the palace of the Marquess of Larios nearby, and I entered a world that I thought no longer existed. I'm talking about the lunch that was served before the meeting began and organized by the air force command, who were occupying the palace. They had gone to a lot of trouble on account of the rank of the guests and because of General Miaja's well-known appreciation of good food. He didn't lose that appreciation even in the last days of the war. Dr. Negrín was also famous for his appetite, which he compensated for by his exceptional vitality.

Although I hadn't had much experience in this kind of meeting, I supposed that if the prime minister himself was presiding no one would lack for anything. What we did lack were all those who had left the country by then. Among them was my old friend General Rojo, who was in France at that point. The same was true of President Azaña, Generals Hernández Saravia, Jurado, Pozas. . . .

The waitresses serving us wore white aprons and caps. The meal was excellent, and I confess I ate it enthusiastically without recalling the rations of my men, made up most recently of nothing but lentils. These memory lapses help to make life bearable. If we were always thinking about all the bad things that are happening or going to happen, we wouldn't be able to go on living.

I ate not only with pleasure but also to excess, subconsciously aware that the next day I would go back to sharing the rations of my troops.

Dr. Negrín presided over the table, and at his right sat Álvarez del Vayo, who was minister of foreign affairs at the time. They were the only civilians at the meeting because, as they told us, it was a council of war. Miaja, who was commander-in-chief of all the land, naval, and air forces, sat on the prime minister's left. Miaja didn't lose his sense of humor during the meal, and he joked with the waitresses, some of whom were very attractive. Around the table, though I don't remember in what order, were General Matallana, chief of the general staff; Colonel Casado, commanding the Army of the Center; General Menéndez, commander of the Army of the Levant; Colonel Moriones, the Marquess of Oroquieta, in command of the Army of Andalusia; Admiral Buiza, commander of the fleet, whom I would have liked to ask why he didn't keep his appointment at Motril; and two colonels who were commanders of the air force. I sat very close to the prime minister because I was the most senior general after Miaja, my promotion having been given retroactive effect to July 19, 1936.

I enjoyed lunch, but when it ended and the council of war began, it didn't take long for indigestion to set in. I hadn't expected it to be pleasant, given our adverse situation, but neither had I expected it to become as tense as it did.

The prime minister asked for the opinion of the four army commanders—Casado, Menéndez, Moriones, and me—as to the possibility of continuing the war, and all four of us were against it. Menéndez, Moriones, and I gave reasons. Casado spoke vehemently, confronting Dr. Negrín.

The minister of foreign affairs confided in us that on that day, February 27, both the French and British governments would go ahead with recognizing Franco's government. This was a bad shock for me, as I had never imagined such a thing might happen. There is no question that I'm naïve about politics.

Prime Minister Negrín and Colonel Casado became embroiled in a fierce argument. The prime minister insisted again and again that under the circumstances, given that Franco would accept only surrender without guarantees of any kind in return, there was no choice but to continue the resistance. Miaja said very little. I think he was suffering from indigestion. I wouldn't have spoken up as much as I did either, if it hadn't been for the fact that the subject affected me very directly.

Álvarez del Vayo explained to us that Franco was negotiating an agreement with Italy to divide up the world supply of mercury, which with a confrontation between the fascist powers and the European democracies would be a hard blow for the latter.

"But to make that agreement Franco needs something he doesn't have yet: the mercury mines at Almadén."

Hearing the name of the place where I had my headquarters, I paid particular attention. I noticed that the participants were looking at me.

"To hold on to that pot of gold," the prime minister interjected, "we have to resist. And we have to make it clear to Franco that, if we have to, we'll blow up the mines at Almadén."

I noticed how intensely everybody was staring at me, especially Dr. Negrín. I don't know what I felt inside or what he expected of me. I only remember that I said, "If the government orders me to blow up the mines at Almadén, I'll obey the order. But I'll do it personally, and when I do I'll be deep inside the mine."

Because I had a reputation for meaning what I say, maybe they thought I would do it. All I know is they stayed quiet. I tried to soften the edge of what I had said by adding, more pleasantly, what became my favorite line from then on: "Gentlemen, when it comes to wars, you have to know how to lose them."

~

The reason for the tension between Prime Minister Negrín and Colonel Casado, which was so striking in the aforementioned meeting at Los Llanos, became clear a few days later. The prime minister was determined to continue the war—so much so that he dedicated himself relentlessly to seeking an alliance with the Communists, who were the only ones as determined as he was. A military junta, the National Defense Council, headed first by Casado and then by Miaja, was formed in Madrid to oppose that alliance. It's not for me to describe what happened there.

Two companies in the Forty-Seventh Brigade of my Army of Extremadura mutinied under the command of Telésforo Aguado, a Communist. They killed their major, García Navarro, a syndicalist I thought highly of, and several more. These deaths at the end of the war, in such a wasteful internal conflict, were terribly sad.

I quickly succeeded in suppressing the conspiracy with a few carefully targeted and timed arrests. The position taken by the commander of the Seventh Army Corps was a great help and particular satisfaction to me. He came to tell me that he was a member of the Communist Party but at the same time that he would never mutiny against me, and he turned out to be as good as his word.

My pen skims swiftly along in writing about such upright people.

In my judgment, the short life of this mutiny shows that what the victors maintain about ours being a Communist army isn't true. I think it's in bad taste and unworthy of an honorable soldier, as I suppose he is, for General Franco to refer to us as the "Red Army" in his final report on the war. The many honorable soldiers who sacrificed their lives to create a regular army, incorporating in its ranks many men who at the beginning of the war were wild revolutionaries, don't deserve such a derogatory description.

I think about many of my Civil Guards, good fathers of families who were paid very little and lost their lives in the battles of Madrid, Brunete, the Ebro, Extremadura. . . . It grieves me to write more.

~

I handed over my army to General Yagüe on March 26, 1939. I tried to deliver it in good order. In our withdrawal from Almadén we collected the region's most notable artistic treasures and deposited them in the Bank of Spain at Ciudad Real, which gave us a receipt. Up to the last minute, I kept a strong guard at the mines in Almadén against the continuing threat of their being blown up. I also saw to the making of an inventory of our armaments, transportation equipment, and heavy materiel.

Once that was done my captain adjutant Pedro Masips made telephone contact with General Yagüe's headquarters to formalize the surrender, in accordance with the orders of the National Defense Council, which was headed in General Miaja's absence by Don Julián Besteiro, a man of firm convictions and great moral courage.

I was summoned to present myself on that March 26, surprised that the place I was told to go to was an open field. I went accompanied only by Captain Masips and, at the wheel, Sergeant Bermúdez. It was his last service to me.

It was very early morning. I approached General Yagüe and, when I was standing before him, executed a regulation salute, which he returned. He was wearing a barracks cap and leather hunting jacket. A squad of his Legionnaires was fifteen paces behind him, standing at ease in their greenish shirts, the sleeves rolled up even though it was a cold morning.

We studied each other curiously. He was younger than I. I don't remember having run across him in the service and knew him only from photographs.

I began to explain the measures I had taken for the proper handover of my army. He gave a quick nod but then immediately interrupted me: "What you've done seems very good, Escobar, but the reason I came in person was to tell you that you're free to leave."

"What did you say?"

"This car, with an escort"—he looked over at the Legionnaires that were guarding it—"will go with you to an airplane that'll take you to Portugal. From there it'll be easy for you to go on to whatever country most suits you."

"Thank you, General, but I'm not going to leave."

"Why?"

"I don't see any reason to."

"Losing the war doesn't seem like much of a reason?"

"When it comes to wars, you have to know how to lose them."

"And who's going to guarantee you," he asked, "that we'll know how to win?"

He said it bitterly. And to leave no doubt about how to interpret that sentence, he told me what had happened to him when he asked for generosity toward the vanquished.

I thanked him for the explanation, but at no time did I think of leaving.

"I began," he insisted, "by telling you that you are free to leave. Now, I'm asking you to do so."

It was a very difficult thing for me, seemingly almost an act of discourtesy, to refuse such a generous offer.

"Your comrades have done it already—Miaja, Casado, Rojo. . . ."

He saw in my face that I wasn't going to yield, and he resigned himself to it.

"All right, then, as you like," he said. "It'll be the last thing I can do for you."

I think these words will turn out to be true.

They took me to Madrid, and while I was in the army's hands I was treated correctly. But when I got to the capital and they put me in the Cisne Prison, as they did with everybody who was being held prisoner in those first days after the end of the war, things were very different.

Finding myself being denied all consideration and courtesy by the jailers, many of whom were civilians, was more painful than I expected. The jailers also relieved me of my uniform.

The cell I'm in now, in Montjuich, seems like a great luxury compared to the cavernous space in which this great multitude of prisoners, military and political, were crowded together and given, all of us, the same treatment.

The only consideration shown me came from the other soldiers who were being held there. That was no small consolation.

I tried to distract myself from all the hardship by reading the Bible, which made very useful reading in that situation. Other prisoners did the same, and I encouraged them to. One day, on account of my deafness and because I was absorbed in my reading, I didn't catch it when a jailer called out my name in the corridor. It was another prisoner who brought it to my attention.

I walked over to the man who had called me; he was waiting for me, looking surly, in an open spot where I would be able to see him.

"Are you Antonio Escobar Huertas?"

My affirmative nod didn't satisfy him.

"Yes or no?"

"Yes, sir."

He certainly knew already who I was because, as if he

had it all set up, he said to me with a malicious smile, "Latrine duty."

As he said it, he pointed to the cleaning equipment that a trusty had set down on the floor. I've never seen slimier or more disgusting buckets and brushes. Although what he expected of me was clear, I resorted to the tactic I use to get some benefit out of my deafness: "What did you say?"

"That you'll be responsible for personally cleaning the toilets for as long as you're here."

A young officer and fellow prisoner, who had been in my army and was acting on natural impulse, bent down over the bucket and said, "I'll help you, General."

It was the wrong thing to do at that moment, because as he bent down the jailer cracked him across the back of the neck with his stick, the way you would to kill a rabbit. The blow sent the young officer head first up against the bucket, opening a gash that began to bleed heavily.

Forgetting my situation and thinking I still had some authority, I took the jailer to task: "Why did you do that?"

He answered me by slapping me in the face with his right hand. It was the first time I had ever been slapped, because my father never hit us. I bled, too, from the corner of my mouth, but not very much.

The soldiers there around us began to shout in protest, but they quieted right down as soon as the jailer called for the guard.

A lot can be said in favor of an opportune slap, and I think that was one for me. It relieved me of all my human vanity. The man who days before was addressed as *Your*

Excellency was now responsible for the lowest duty in the prison.

I took the bucket and brush, and the jailer explained to me, very spitefully, "Your people had my father—who was an honorable soldier and not a traitor like you—cleaning the latrines in the Modelo Prison for three months. Then they shot him without a trial."

"I'm sorry," I said.

"It's too late to be sorry!"

He didn't understand me. I was sorry about a lot of things, among them that they had given his father such treatment but also that the jailer should have found some recompense in doing the same thing to me three years later.

~

Even the worst episodes in the war were interrupted by something that justified a smile. Except when they told me about José's death.

So I went to the latrines and began working, not all that effectively because I wasn't used to manual labor. The prison chaplain appeared in this very inappropriate place. He put out his hand to say hello and I did the same, but I then pulled it back because it was so dirty. The priest didn't let me pull it away and forcefully took my hand, so I was able to kiss his.

"I'm sorry about your situation, Colonel."

"Don't worry about it, Father."

"I'll do whatever I can for you, but these are hard times."

I don't see priests as pests the way their detractors among the people do, but I know they are inclined to ask favors, and this one, I saw, needed one from me.

"Colonel, there are inevitably going to be executions in these circumstances. . . ."

He stopped, waiting for me to agree, but I didn't say anything. Still he went on, "Even if they've forgotten how to practice their faith, a lot of the men condemned to death are Catholics. And I can't help them much at that point."

I knew this and so did the others, many of whom were spending their lives waiting for the short trials that would end them. Compared to those trials, mine is a model of justice even if it is very summary. And yet, after such a sad statement, the explanation he gave me for it brought a smile to my face: "I can't help them because they say I'm a fascist priest."

"And are you?"

"Like hell I am!"

This was language that the priests in my Army of Extremadura didn't use. The man realized he had gone out of bounds and begged my pardon with an explanation: "Excuse me, Colonel, but I've spent the whole war as a chaplain in the Legion."

This was the first time I had been given something to laugh about since being put in prison.

He told me he was trying to recruit priests from outside the prison. Some of them were teachers in the schools where the men who were shot had studied as children.

"But there are nights when they don't give me time to send for anybody."

Although all the sentences were imposed after a trial, some of the trials were so short, and were followed so immediately by execution, that they weren't all that different from the shameful "walks" that were perpetrated at the beginning of the war by the revolutionaries on our side.

"You can help me a lot, Colonel. You have more influence over them than I do."

"All right, Father. I'll tell them you're a priest who uses cuss words but you aren't a fascist."

I say I laughed because a man can't always be crying, but this conversation couldn't have been sadder. For all their arguments, I still think the victors have turned the Christian faith into a social creed. I'm afraid that won't be good for our religion in the long run.

I helped the chaplain with pleasure, but it took a considerable effort. There's a lot of ignorance about religion even among people who are well educated in other sciences. They had a hard time accepting the idea that, although the chaplain was a Francoist priest, that made him no less a priest when it came to granting absolution. I suffered a good deal, but there also were compensations. The main one was seeing how, when it was time for the last rites offered us by our Mother the Church, it was a rare Catholic who didn't receive them in happiness and peace.

In the month I spent in that prison, I believe I took part in about a hundred cases involving a death sentence followed by execution. Even the ones who didn't want spiritual aid were grateful for my intention. It's wrongheaded not to offer such a significant helping hand, out of simple human respect, to somebody who is about to leave this life.

The few military and political leaders who didn't accept exile were there together in the Cisne Prison. There weren't too many of us. I had the honor of meeting Professor Besteiro there. He succeeded Pablo Iglesias as the leader of the Socialist Party. We comforted each other, because like me he rejected the anarchists' atrocities, to the point that during the war, as a protest, he dropped out of politics altogether. He nevertheless took on the thankless task of losing it, becoming president of the National Defense Council when General Miaja left for France. Professor Besteiro had the courage to stay in Madrid to await the arrival of the victors. I haven't heard anything about him since I came to Barcelona.

Professor Besteiro is a very agreeable and well-spoken man. The few times we had the chance to talk during those days, he described to me his various efforts to make peace between the two sides. He traveled to France and England in the process, but he always came back from his trips, even though he could have used his precarious health as an excuse for staying there. Maybe that's why I got along so well with him. Obviously, he didn't get any results in his attempts to make peace. It's clear that the only peace the victors wanted is the one we have.

~

I was glad when they told me I was being transferred to Barcelona because I knew my son Antonio was a prisoner in this castle. I thought the prison routine would be like the one in Madrid, which in all its slackness had the virtue of making it possible for the inmates to have contact with each other.

That's not how it's been here. I came here to be tried and, what's more, as the senior and highest-ranking soldier of all of us who served in the Army of the Republic. I suppose that's why they've kept me in solitary confinement, and so strictly that I can't see my son Antonio. Soon, when my sentence is final, I'll be able to see him.

I've taken notes of my trial and also of my first conversations with my counsel, Andrés Sierra Valverde, a lawyer who is deeply experienced in this sort of trial because he has practiced before the People's Tribunals as well as in the nationalist courts-martial. He has defended about two thousand defendants in the latter. I've come to care for him from the bottom of my heart. Even though he's currently carrying a crushing work load, he gives me particular attention and, above all, affection and respect. But it has been clear from the day we met in the locutorium of the castle that he doesn't hope to win my case, just to save my life.

"We have to conduct our defense," he told me, "in such a way as to avoid the supreme penalty."

"So that I'll be absolved?"

"No, Colonel, I didn't say that. I'm saying that we can fight to avoid a capital sentence, or persuade them to accompany it, if they do impose it, with language in favor of a pardon."

In all sincerity and even humility, he admitted to me that in the many and various trials he has participated in, he has hardly ever won an exculpatory judgment, but he said he has secured commutation of the death sentence. It seems to be the case that the overall sentencing scheme has been worked out by Franco himself, which is why the outcome is so prejudicial to the defendant.

"Don't delude yourself, Don Andrés. They're going to shoot me. I'm so convinced of it that I've been preparing myself to die ever since I set foot in this castle." Actually, since even before that: ever since I decided to hand myself over at the head of my army, and if I had any doubt about it, General Yagüe was very explicit with me that he could do no better for me than what he had done.

That statement came as a bucket of cold water to my counsel, because he understood it as meaning that I didn't want to live. I assured him very strenuously of the contrary, that I did want to live, although I emphasized that I didn't see how to make it happen. At that he recovered his spirits and explained to me, in great detail and with very evident learning, that from the creation of the Civil Guard in 1844 until 1936 there have been thirty military revolts, but our Corps hasn't participated in any of them. "The Civil Guard never rebels!" he concluded with an enthusiasm that wasn't contagious. I don't agree that my being part of an institution will take me in one direction or another, unless I want it to.

"So what am I, a rebel or a prisoner of war? Because I don't know of any law that permits the execution of prisoners of war."

"According to the new jurisprudence, you're not a prisoner of war, you're a rebel."

"Why? Because I fought against the rebellion, I'm a rebel? That's a ridiculous contradiction."

"Colonel, your theory's a contradiction—of history. The rebellion's been redeemed by victory."

This last sentence angered me beyond measure, and I blurted out a stupid piece of foolishness. "Standing here before my open grave, I assure you that I'd rather contradict history than my conscience."

I say it was a piece of foolishness because I've seen a lot of atrocities committed in this war on the pretext of obeying one's conscience. But that my grave was open before me, and still is, I have very little doubt.

In order not to complicate my defense, which was already hard enough for him, I changed the subject and asked him earnestly to get permission for me to see my son Antonio, and he told me in great distress that wasn't in his power. To make up for that, he promised to argue that I should be allowed to appear in the court-martial in my Corps uniform, as I've been doing since then.

~

There's not much to say about the court-martial. Here in my solitude, going over it in my mind, I magnify what each of us said. But all of it, put on paper, doesn't take up any more space than that death sentence of the soldier in the Toral Group that caused me so much trouble. It seems to be a prevailing evil in this war to judge men in a rush and then write out the sentence without much concern for syntactical niceties.

They condemn me to death for military rebellion, with aggravating circumstances. The sentence has to be ratified by higher authority, and it will be final when the captain general of the Fourth Region, General Orgaz, approves it. My pardon, for which several people are exerting themselves, is a separate matter.

I focus in my notes on the prosecutor's inappropriately taking up the subject of our religion. He didn't seem to be very well versed in it. He asked me, "As a soldier, and with your family background, you could fight side by side with people who had no God and no fatherland?"

"If I believed God wasn't with those poor people I'd be the most wretched of men."

"You're not answering my question, Colonel."

"I don't know how to answer it any other way. My religion doesn't permit me to believe that God is with one specific group of people and excludes everyone else."

The prosecutor didn't care much about my relationship with God, and the only reason he got into it, as I've already described, was as an excuse to go over the episode of the monastery on Calle Lauria, which he thought was very prejudicial to me. I was highly offended by the impression that his reference to the episode was received by the court with satisfaction, not out of malice but as a justification for the preordained sentence they had to impose. So I felt I had to rebut the prosecutor along the following lines, taken from my notes: "What happened on the night between July 19 and 20 in that monastery was the fault of those who had rebelled that day and who today constitute the government. They're absolved by their victory, as I understand it, but by their rebellion they weakened the state and set the stage for the anarchist revolution against which I tried to fight with all my might, as I did against the uprising, in fulfillment of my obligations as a soldier and my oath to the legally constituted government."

It was the only time the president of the court-martial took me to task intemperately, warning me that I wasn't there to make accusations but to defend myself. I think he took the opportunity to speed up the adjournment of the trial, returning again and again to what the record showed had already been said by me and the witnesses. The prosecutor made one final statement, repeating what he had said before, and my counsel warmly defended me as a person, recalling my good record before July 18, 1936. He gave the impression that I had been such an excellent soldier until that date that I deserved to be forgiven for what I had done thereafter. He also defended the Civil Guard, and that pleased me.

Before adjourning the trial the president asked me, "Do you have anything more to say that hasn't been said by the defendant himself or his counsel?"

"I want to thank the court for the courtesy it's shown me throughout."

I noticed a distrustful reaction to this among its members, as if there had been a double meaning in what I said. There hadn't. After so many months of humiliation, basically at the prison in Madrid, and of solitude in my cell at Montjuich, it was a relief to be treated courteously by those who were sitting in judgment on me. Sometimes I even noticed that they were interested in what I was saying, and went so far as to show a touch of understanding. I thanked them for that even though I knew they could do very little for me because they were acting in the line of duty and under orders. That may not be the way those who sit in judgment should act, but I think it's hard to avoid it, particularly after such a cruel war.

"I especially want to thank my counsel for his defense

of the Civil Guard, and his demonstration that it's never rebelled in all its history and didn't do so in this war: of the six generals who were in the Civil Guard's ranks when the uprising broke out, all six remained loyal to the legal government."

Maybe it was because I had spent months in silence that I spoke more than I usually did. The president made a gesture toward adjourning the trial, and I had time to say only, "But even if that hadn't been so, I would never have rebelled. The truth is the truth even if only a minority upholds it. Even if it's a minority of one."

~

I apologized to my counsel after the trial. I have a feeling that some of what I said in the court-martial could be interpreted as a criticism of his defense. But I don't think he took it that way. He's clear in his mind that the position he took in my defense was, legally, the only one possible, but it seems natural to him that I should want to express my own point of view. Not only does it not bother him, I can say now that he presses for my life as hard as he can, and toward that end he has sent a telegram to the minister of the army, and a petition to the head of state, for the commutation of my death sentence.

"Your sister-in-law, in Madrid," meaning Ramón's wife, "is making very great efforts. Although I haven't had an answer to the telegram I sent to General Varela, she tells me she's been able to talk to him and thinks he's inclined to intervene in favor of commuting the sentence."

"And to what would they commute it?"

"To this: thirty years in prison."

I do the arithmetic, which tells me I could live that long. According to my father, we're a long-lived family, except for the ones who die of bullet wounds. He told us he had a grandfather in Alvaredo who lived to be over a hundred.

I've had visitors since my solitary confinement was lifted. The first was of course Antonio, and every day I see his wife Angelita, who has come to live in Barcelona to be nearer her husband. Antonio is very thin and therefore seems taller. He is very sad. Angelita tells me that my situation is unbearable for him. I never thought he loved me that much. I've sometimes even thought he drifted away from me, because he married very young and lived his life apart. And also, as I've said, he is a little arrogant because he has been such an outstanding soldier, a graduate of the academy in Toledo and not someone who has risen through the ranks from buck sergeant, like me. The poor boy has lost at least his military career, forever. In the prime of life. You have to be a soldier to feel what that means. I don't know how it benefits Spain to lose a good soldier like Antonio. Discarding me, even so abruptly, is less absurd because at my age I can't serve very long.

Angelita tells me . . . Angelita tells me a lot of things I would rather not know. My brother Alfredo went over to the nationalist zone at the beginning of 1937. He entered it at the border in Irún, where he was subjected to reeducation. They made him a lieutenant colonel in the Civil Guard and assigned him to the command of a division in Asturias. At the end of the war on April 1, 1939, he was separated from the Corps by decree for disaffection with the regime. How can it be that after all his suffering in that embassy, after risking so much by going over to the other side, after spending the whole war risking his life in missions in the mountains of Asturias, he should be separated from the service for disaffection with the regime? I asked Angelita how my brother reacted, and she told me he just says, "Franco knows what's best." I marvel at the great influence this man has on those who've served under him. I hope he uses it well.

And Angelita tells me that my daughter Emilia has come back from Italy. She was so tenaciously persistent, as sisters are in pursuit of their goals, that she was received by Franco and fell at his feet, begging for my life. He was moved by my daughter's tears, so I'm told, to the point that his own eyes moistened, too. I'm grateful to him for that, because I think it must have served as some consolation for my little Emilia. Very sensibly, the prioress of her convent doesn't want her to come visit while we still don't know what's going to happen to me. The Sisters of Adoration intercede in many cases, and they say their account has a positive balance in this one because of the many services I've rendered. I don't remember what they might be. I ask Angelita to tell them that where their intercession will do me the most good is in the court of heaven. "You still have your sense of humor, Father," she says. They don't know that I say it very seriously.

Tears came to Franco's eyes, but he said that what happened to me wasn't up to him. He meant that approval of the sentence was the responsibility of the captain general, General Orgaz. God forgive me, but when it comes to mounting a coup General Orgaz is the general to do it, par excellence. As a fervent monarchist, he participated in every coup attempt from 1932 on, following the proclamation of the Republic. He finally hit upon the right one. For him, legality consists of coming to power by insurrection. He couldn't possibly refuse to approve the sentence, because that wouldn't fit with his way of thinking.

Although I'm not too concerned about what happens to my body, because I know Angelita will be the one who looks after it, I've made one comment to her about it. It's a custom among Franciscan tertiaries to be buried in the Franciscan habit. The way things stand, I would rather they buried me in my Civil Guard uniform.

~

I don't know what I felt inside when they told me that two nuns were waiting for me in the locutorium. I was sure they were my daughter and my sister Dolores and their visit could have meant several things, but suffering was in any event inevitable. I felt less sorry for Lola, but I preferred that my daughter, Emilia, remember me as I was the last time I saw her, when she took her final vows and I wore the dress uniform of the Corps—blue, trimmed with gold.

The sergeant told me it wasn't my daughter who had asked for the visit, and I continued to be in the dark until I saw Magdalena, whom I recognized immediately despite her wimple and the severity of her habit.

This war, the end of which for me I see now so near,

has held no grief that wasn't relieved by a touch of humor, and for me at that moment it was finding myself with Magdalena in such peculiar circumstances.

"They didn't know how to explain what this visit was about. And they said there were two sisters that wanted to see me."

Magdalena, visibly upset, gestured toward the other sister, who had held herself somewhat apart from us.

"Ah, of course. Sisters always go in pairs, like the Civil Guard."

She laughed, but with an effort, because when women are on the verge of tears it doesn't do any good to joke with them. I had no choice, though, because I, too, was struggling inside.

"Do you remember when I told you that being a sister is as important as being a member of the Civil Guard?"

Magdalena showed a trace of Andalusian lightness, despite the difficulty of the moment. "No, Colonel, you told me it was more important."

It so happens that Sister Anunciación, the sister who received me in the Ritz Hotel with a certain mistrust when I still didn't know about Magdalena's situation, is now the provincial of their order in Catalonia. She brought Magdalena along with her in her new position, because I suppose after so many years they were uncommonly close to each other. You could compare them to Sergeant Bermúdez and me. It was Sister Anunciación who had sent Magdalena to visit me. These sisters who've lived through the war with the Reds have become very liberal.

"Mother Anunciación has asked me to tell you that all our community prays for you."

"That's very good."

"We're also petitioning that . . . that . . ."

Because my visitors were hesitating on this point I helped them out of their predicament.

"That I be pardoned?"

"That, yes. A mother of the order has an uncle who is a lieutenant colonel of the border guards, very influential . . ."

She said it so ingenuously that, in order to avoid being more moved than I had to be, I scolded her: "Sister, a lieutenant colonel of the border guard can't save the life of a general! Don't you see that? You don't do me justice."

"We do what we can."

"Of course. And you do it very well, especially in praying for me. But leave the border guard in peace."

She insisted again that Mother Anunciación is very grateful to me. I suppose it was because I hadn't interfered in Magdalena's taking her final vows. As if I could have done anything else.

"Mother wanted you to know that we don't forget you in these moments. That's why she allowed me to come."

"Of course, of course."

"Otherwise, it's not customary in our order to make visits."

"I would guess not. Just as it's not customary to shake hands in saying good-bye. Although on that point I might have been misled, because Mother Anunciación explained that it depends on the circumstances."

This was a ploy to avoid prolonging the conversation. Magdalena, her eyes shrouded, began to put out her hand, but I put mine behind my back.

"And this time the circumstances aren't propitious. Good-bye, Magdalena. May God repay you."

I thought her very pale, but as beautiful as ever. I was glad, because I would like it if all sisters were beautiful. My daughter Emilia is.

~

AUTHOR'S EPILOGUE

General Escobar was shot by a firing squad in the moat of the castle of Montjuich on February 8, 1940.

On the morning of February 7, the presiding judge in the case, Major Monteys, summoned the general's counsel, Don Andrés Sierra Valverde, to inform him that the sentence had been approved in Madrid and that he had the required order in his possession. The major said that the sentence would be carried out the same night, and that, as had been requested by the defense, military honors would be rendered to the prisoner in the course of the execution. It was the first time such a privilege had been granted to a prisoner who was condemned to death.

The prisoner's counsel, having changed into his military uniform from the civilian clothes he usually wore when he visited his client, went to the castle in the afternoon to communicate the news to him. When General Escobar saw his counsel in uniform, he understood its significance and asked him, "What's happening?"

"Just confirmation of the sentence, Colonel."

"All right. What do we need to do?"

The general was taken to the office of the commandant of the castle, where were gathered the presiding judge in the case, the secretary, the commandant himself, and soldier guards.

The judge proceeded with the reading of the sentence while everyone present remained standing. When the prisoner learned that he was to be rendered military honors at the moment of execution, he gave his counsel a grateful look and at the end of the reading went to him and embraced him. He then leaned over the table in the office and signed the sentence with his first name and two surnames. In the space above his signature, before signing, he wrote: "God's will be done." With his customary courtesy, as this was a departure from regulation procedure, he begged the pardon of the judge for having written it.

Two trucks bearing fifty Civil Guards drove up to the castle under the command of a captain, who signed a receipt for the prisoner and took him into custody to take him to the chapel. The captain came to attention before the general, who returned his salute as he said to him, "I hope you and your men will do your work very carefully, Captain. I'm not a man who's given to dying from bullet wounds."

His statement wasn't understood by those present. The general was referring to the wounds he received during the war, which would have been presumed mortal but for the fact that they hadn't ended his life.

His son Antonio, who was serving his own sentence in the castle, was waiting for his father at the door to the chapel, and they hugged each other tightly and sadly.

Don Andrés Sierra Valverde returned to the castle at three in the morning, accompanied by Angelita, Antonio's wife and therefore the general's daughter-in-law.

The general made his confession to the chaplain and received extreme unction. He then spoke with his son and daughter-in-law. In his later account, Antonio Escobar Valtierra specifically said that his father, in his last words, urged his son insistently not to harbor any hatred or rancor against anyone on account of his death. He extracted a promise to that effect. The son admits in all humility that he's not sure he has unfailingly kept that promise.

A Mass was celebrated at four in the morning, which was attended by several officer-prisoners in the castle. The general followed the Mass closely in his missal.

According to his defense counsel, who was present at the Mass, the general received Communion "with a fervor that was devoid of sentimentality".

Until the moment he was called to his execution he prayed before an image of the Virgin that surmounted the altar.

He bid farewell to his son and daughter-in-law with loving kisses.

He went to the place of execution, which was the courtyard of the castle, accompanied by the chaplain and his counsel and escorted by the members of the Civil Guard.

The infantry corporal leading the firing squad to the moat took a wrong turn, generating confusion and delay. The general, who was wearing his uniform jacket, asked that an orderly be sent to bring him a coat. "This is taking time," he said, "and it's cold. I don't want to shiver, and have them think it's out of fear."

This was done, and he put the coat on with the help

of his defense counsel and the chaplain. Dawn began to break, and the general said, "Soon it'll be day."

"Yes, my son," the chaplain said, "and you will see the face of God."

"Be it so, Father."

When they finally situated him in the right place for his execution, the chaplain handed him a crucifix and then, with the general's defense counsel, drew away.

A short lieutenant from the reserve ranks was in command of the firing squad. He approached the general and begged his pardon.

"Fulfill your duty," the general said, to calm him.

The lieutenant did so, giving the command for half the firing squad to assume a kneeling position. The general, keeping the upper portion of his body very erect, knelt at the same time as the first rank of the firing squad.

The general's son, Antonio Escobar Valtierra, says that he heard the shots from his cell and that, despite the forty-three years that have passed since then, he cannot rid his memory of that moment. When he describes it, his eyes cloud over with tears. The general's son, despite his age, retains a fine appearance.

A military doctor attended the execution, and after the shots were fired he approached the general's body, which still showed signs of life. The doctor pointed to the general's temple so that the lieutenant commanding the firing squad would give him the coup de grâce, which he did.

The body nevertheless continued to move, and the doctor became agitated. He urgently directed the lieutenant to fire a second coup de grâce directly into the heart, which ended the general's life

The fifty Civil Guards, preceded by a band of trumpets and drums and marching by threes past the body of General Escobar, rendered it military honors.

~

TRANSLATOR'S GLOSSARY OF PERSONS AND ORGANIZATIONS

What follows omits individuals and organizations about whom little if anything need be added to what is said about them in the text; the material included there is generally not repeated here. Persons and entities named in small capitals within an entry are themselves the subject of an entry.

The full name of each person is given in alphabetical order, family name first (normally that of the person's father, by which the person is generally known), followed by the mother's family name and then by the person's given name or names. For example, ANTONIO (his given name) ESCOBAR (his own and his father's family name) HUERTAS (his mother's family name) would appear as Escobar Huertas, Antonio.

AGUADO RONCO, TELÉSFORO (?–Spring 1939). A republican major in command of the Forty-Seventh Mixed Brigade, he holed up in the mountains near Los Navalmorales (province of Toledo) in March 1939, to carry on the war as a guerilla. He subsisted there for two or three months on petty thefts and provisions supplied by his wife and daughter during visits he paid them periodically in the valley below. His wife's brother, a member of the FALANGE, encountered him one night in their village and shot him dead.

ALFONSO XIII (1886–1941). King of Spain from birth, his father Alfonso XII having died before he was born, Alfonso XIII left Spain in April 1931 and settled into exile in Rome. He did not abdicate from the throne, however, until January 1941. His grandson became king of Spain as Juan Carlos I in the transition to democracy after FRANCO's death. Juan Carlos abdicated in 2014 in favor of his son, who is currently King of Spain as Felipe VI.

ÁLVAREZ DEL VAYO Y OLLOQUI, JULIO (1891–1975). A fellow traveler of the COMMUNISTS, he fled Spain at the end of the war and lived in exile in Mexico, the United States, and Switzerland. He continued to be active in leftist politics from abroad until his death in Geneva.

ALZUGARAY GOICOECHEA, EMILIO (1880–1944). He had retired from the army before the war, but when it broke out he volunteered for the republican side in command of the Basque Antifascist Militias. After recovering from grave wounds sustained during the battle for Madrid, he was given command of the Second Army Corps, with which he suffered a disastrous loss operating between the Garabitas and Cerro del Águila. He was demoted and sidelined for the rest of the war, and at its end he went into exile in southern France. There, in 1944, he was arrested as a spy by the Gestapo and killed by the French Resistance when it attacked a convoy in which he was traveling as the Gestapo's prisoner. A square is named after him in Melilla.

ANARCHISTS, ANARCHO-SYNDICALISTS, Anarchism is a political philosophy and movement that arose in France during the nineteenth century and spread throughout Europe with the aim of using violence and even terror to overthrow the established political, economic, and social order and government generally. Spain was a stronghold of deeply and violently anticlerical anarchism, especially in Catalonia and Andalusia. Anarcho-syndicalists were anarchists who saw labor unions as the best vehicle for direct action by the working class to abolish the capitalist order and to establish in its place a social order based on workers organized in production units. See CNT, FAI.

ARANDA MATA, ANTONIO (1888–1979). A nationalist FREEMASON who earned promotion and fame in Morocco and the siege of Oviedo before the war, he participated in several of its most important engagements. After it ended he plotted in favor of a restoration of the monarchy and was confined to Mallorca in 1946. He was forced to retire three years later.

ARANGUREN ROLDÁN, JOSÉ (1875–1939). Promoted by the REPUBLIC to general of the CIVIL GUARD four months before the outbreak of the war, he refused at its end to flee from Spain. Like General Escobar, Aranguren had a son who died in the war fighting for the nationalist side. FRANCO, when he was told that Aranguren's injury would make it impossible for him to stand during his execution, is said to have replied by ordering that he be shot even if he was on a stretcher.

ASCASO ABADÍA, FRANCISCO (1901–1936). An anarcho-syndicalist, he led the July 20, 1936, attack on the Atarazanas Barracks (with DURRUTI) and died doing so.

ASSAULT GUARDS. A corps of urban police formed by the REPUBLIC in 1932 and disbanded by FRANCO at the end of the war.

AYGUADÉ Y MIRÓ, ARTEMI (1889–1946). He went into exile in Mexico after the war and spent the rest of his life there.

AZAÑA Y DÍAZ, MANUEL (1880–1940). Strongly antimonarchist and anticlerical, Azaña was a long-time republican politician and one of the organizers of the POPULAR FRONT. When it won the February 16, 1936, elections, he became prime minister of the REPUBLIC (for the second time) and then its president three months later. He occupied that post for all but two months of the war, struggling with limited success to unite the many contending republican factions, until he resigned on March 3, 1939, after crossing the Pyrenees into France on foot. It remains controversially unclear whether he received the sacraments before he died there in November 1940.

BATET MESTRES, DOMINGO (1872–1937). Batet was a career soldier whose execution is said to have been ordered by FRANCO in revenge for the bad light in which Batet had cast him in an official report in 1921. Shortly before he was executed he wrote a letter to his children enjoining them to "be good citizens and do your duty whatever may be the circumstances fate holds in store for you."

BERMÚDEZ, SERGEANT. A fictitious character designed by the author to represent the average soldier. Bermúdez is a foil for General Escobar, an example of what the latter might have been had he not risen from his initial rank of "buck sergeant" to colonel and then general.

BESTEIRO FERNÁNDEZ, JULIÁN (1870–1940). At the end of the war, Besteiro was arrested and court-martialed by the nationalists and sentenced to thirty years in prison. He died there after serving a little more than one year.

BOSCH GIMPERA, PERE (1891–1974). An archeologist and professor of ancient and medieval history at the University of Barcelona, he served as rector of the university from 1933 to 1939. He also served as counselor of justice of the GENERALITAT. Going into exile in Mexico when the war ended, he held university chairs there and in Guatemala after 1941.

BROTONS GÓMEZ, FRANCISCO (?–1939). General Escobar's comrade and fellow colonel of the CIVIL GUARD when the war broke out, he was executed by firing squad a week before the war ended.

BUIZA FERNÁNDEZ-PALACIOS, MIGUEL (1898–1963). At the end of the war Buiza was the admiral in command of the republican fleet, the remains of which he delivered in March 1939 to the French at Bizerte, Tunisia, despite NEGRÍN's orders to the contrary. Buiza's remaining years included a period of service in the French Foreign Legion, working as a bookseller or hotel accountant (the record is unclear) in Oran, participating in the Allies' campaign for Tunisia during World War II, living in France for a brief period after that war, then assuming the name Moshe Blum in 1947 and volunteering as the captain of a ship that transported Holocaust survivors to Palestine. In this latter role he was arrested by the British and held for a time in a concentration camp in Haifa. He resumed his identity as Miguel Buiza upon his release and returned to Oran, then emigrated to Marseille to live out his remaining years. He died in Marseilles.

(FERNÁNDEZ) BURRIEL, ÁLVARO (1879–1936). At his court-martial after the uprising that set off the war, echoing GODED (they were tried together), Burriel said he rebelled not against the REPUBLIC but against anarchy. He was executed by a firing squad in Montjuich on August 12, 1936. (His family name is shown here in parentheses because he went by his mother's name rather than his father's. That practice is not exceptional where the father's family name is a common one.)

CABANELLAS FERRER, MIGUEL (1872–1938). As the senior general and president of the nationalists' COUNCIL OF NATIONAL DEFENSE, he was the lone dissenter from its decision, early in the war, to proclaim FRANCO the leader of the nationalists. Cabanellas then served as chief inspector of the army until his death a little more than seven months later.

CALVO SOTELO, JOSÉ (1893–1936). Calvo Sotelo was a prominent right-wing politician whose assassination on July 16, 1936, was blamed by the right on the republican government and was an important spark (or perhaps pretext) for the war. He had served as finance minister during the dictatorship of Miguel Primo de

Rivera and was exiled early in the REPUBLIC, but he returned in May 1934 and was a leader of the opposition in the CORTES when he was assassinated. FRANCO honored his memory by making him the first Duke of Calvo Sotelo in 1948.

CAMPESINO, EL. See GONZÁLEZ GONZÁLEZ, VALENTÍN.

CARLISTS. The Carlists wanted to see the restoration of the monarchy, but in the person of a descendant of Fernando VII's brother Don Carlos because in their view Isabel II, as a female, had been ineligible to inherit the throne. Profoundly traditionalist and ultra-Catholic, the Carlists were even more conservative than the Alfonsine MONARCHISTS.

CARMELITES. A contemplative order of monks founded in the thirteenth century on Mount Carmel.

CARTHUSIANS. A cloistered order of monks and nuns founded in the eleventh century in Chartreuse, France.

CASADO LÓPEZ, SEGISMUNDO (1893–1968). A longtime professional soldier, Casado is most notable for having led a coup against NEGRÍN so the war could be ended. Just before the end came, Casado fled by ship to Marseille and from there went into exile in the United Kingdom, Venezuela, and Colombia. In 1961 he returned to Spain, where he underwent a court-martial that cleared him of any crime but did not permit him to rejoin the military. His efforts to obtain a pension and have his rank reinstated came to an unsuccessful end in 1966. In the time that remained to him, he published his memoirs under the title *Así cayó Madrid* (The Fall of Madrid).

CASTRO DELGADO, ENRIQUE (1907–1965). He fled to France at the end of the war and then went into exile in the Soviet Union, where he represented the PCE in the Comintern. Disillusioned, he left for Mexico after World War II. There he wrote a book titled *Mi fe se perdió en Moscú*, (I Lost My Faith in Moscow), which was virulently critical of prominent republicans such as LA PASIONARIA, LISTER, and MODESTO (and described by one source as "a kick in the *cojones*" full of black humor, contempt, mockery, and accusations that named names). Castro returned to Spain in 1964 and died at the very beginning of 1965.

CEDA (full name in Spanish: Confederación Española de Derechos Autónomas; in English: Spanish Confederation of the Autonomous Right). A political alliance of right-wing Catholic parties formed in 1933 with the aim of defending Christian civilization and other conservative values, it lost many members to the FALANGE in the months before the war. FRANCO dissolved it in April 1937 when he merged it into the MOVEMENT.

CIVIL GUARD (in Spanish: Guardia Civil). Founded as a national police force, it is a paramilitary body commanded by an army general as part of the Ministry of Interior. Widely respected for its discipline, esprit de corps, and devotion to duty—*Todo por la patria* (All for the fatherland) and *El honor es mi divisa* (Honor is my badge) are its mottos—it has also been feared and even hated by some Spaniards as a state instrument of oppression.

CNT (full name in Spanish: Confederación Nacional de Trabajo; in English: National Confederation of Labor). A confederation of ANARCHO-SYNDICALIST labor unions formed in 1910, it was outlawed during the FRANCO dictatorship but carried on its activities clandestinely and from exile. Legalized again in the transition to democracy, it is still in existence.

COMMITTEE OF ANTIFASCIST MILITIAS. A body established by decree of the GENERALITAT on July 21, 1936, to enforce public order in Catalonia. It was dissolved on October 1, 1936.

COMMUNIST PARTY OF SPAIN (in Spanish: Partido Comunista de España, generally known by its initials PCE). A political party established in 1921 by dissident members of the SOCIALIST PARTY, it was an important part of the POPULAR FRONT. The Soviet Union controlled the PCE throughout the war. The military support provided by the Soviets to the REPUBLIC, and the Communists' disciplined approach to the conduct of the war, gave them great influence in the republican government, especially during NEGRÍN's tenure as prime minister.

COMPANYS I JOVER, LLUÍS (1882–1940). Companys was a lawyer, leader of the Republican Left Party of Catalonia, and president of the GENERALITAT beginning in 1934 and throughout the war. When it ended, he fled to France. Shortly after France fell to German occupation in June 1940, he was detained by the Gestapo, which turned him over to the FRANCO regime in early September. Preston says Companys was held in Montjuich "in solitary confinement and tortured and beaten. Senior figures of the regime visited his cell, insulted him and threw coins or crusts of bread at him." After a summary court-martial that lasted less than an hour, he was executed eight months and a week after General Escobar's execution. Companys heard Mass and received Communion on the day of his execution, in which he faced the firing squad without a blindfold. As they fired, he cried *¡Per Catalunya!* (For Catalonia!). "The cause of death," Preston says, "was cynically given as 'traumatic internal haemorrhage'."

CORTES. The Spanish parliament.

COUNCIL OF NATIONAL DEFENSE (in Spanish: Junta de Defensa Nacional). The committee established by the nationalists on July 24, 1936, with nine generals and two colonels as its members, to carry on the work of government. Beevor calls it a "figurehead establishment" because it soon vested FRANCO with the ultimate power to govern.

DÍAZ SANDINO, FELIPE (1891–1960). He fled to France when the war ended and spent the rest of his life in exile there and in the Dominican Republic, Colombia, and Chile.

DURRUTI DUMANGE, JOSÉ BUENAVENTURA (1896–1936). The most popular ANARCHIST leader, Durruti died during the battle for Madrid when a comrade's pistol fired accidentally after being caught in a car door. For morale and propaganda reasons, the anarchists claimed he had been killed by a sniper. For his funeral in Barcelona, hundreds of thousands of mourners lined the streets.

ESCOFET ALSINA, FEDERICO (1898–1987). He had been condemned to death by the REPUBLIC for his part in the 1934 uprising for Catalan independence, but his sentence was commuted to thirty years, of which he served two before being granted amnesty when the POPULAR FRONT came to power in 1936. After serving in several battles (including Belchite, where he was wounded, and Teruel), at the end of the war he crossed into France with COMPANYS and went into exile in Belgium. He returned to Spain after FRANCO died and lived in Barcelona until his own death.

FAI (full name in Spanish: Federación Anarquista Ibérica; in English: Iberian Anarchist Federation). The activist wing of the CNT, the FAI was an extreme ANARCHIST movement that saw the REPUBLIC as an instrument of the ruling class, like the monarchy. In strikes, street fighting, and uprisings, the FAI favored and practiced violence over political action. It still exists today, but its membership is secret.

FALANGE ESPAÑOLA DE LAS JONS (the last word being the initials of Juntas de Ofensiva Nacional-Sindicalista). An extreme-right, corporatist, fascist-style political party known generally as La Falange (which literally means "the Phalanx"), it was founded in 1933 by JOSÉ ANTONIO PRIMO DE RIVERA. After the war it went through a transformation (see NATIONAL MOVEMENT) and name change to Falange Española Tradicionalista y de las Juntas de Ofensiva Nacional Sindicalista. A remnant of it still exists today, but it has no representation in the CORTES and little if any effect on Spanish public life.

FRANCISCANS. A leading order of mendicant friars, nuns, and tertiaries founded by Saint Francis of Assisi in thirteenth-century Italy.

FRANCO BAHAMONDE, FRANCISCO (1892–1975). Born in Ferrol (in Galicia), he was descended from a long line of Spanish naval officers but could not become one himself because entry to the Spanish naval academy was closed from 1906 to 1913. Joining the army instead, he became the youngest general in Europe at the age of thirty-three and was Spain's most prestigious military officer when the rebellion broke out. He did not join it until just before the uprising on July 17, 1936. As General Escobar notes, Franco was regarded as an exceptionally capable military strategist. He is often described as astute, shrewd, cunning, courageous, manipulative, vindictive, driven, ruthless, lucky, and ambitious. His brother Ramón is quoted by Preston as saying, "Look, Paco's so ambitious that he'd be capable of murdering our mother and, I suppose, our father." The COUNCIL OF NATIONAL DEFENSE all but unanimously named him head of state and general-in-chief (*Generalísimo*) on October 1, 1936. The statute of the FALANGE, as revised after the NATIONAL MOVEMENT was established, provided that, as *Caudillo* (which means "Leader" on the model of Hitler's *Führer* and Mussolini's *Duce*), Franco would be "responsible only to God and to History". He retained his power as Spain's dictator until the day he died. The fact that he moderated its exercise somewhat in the latter part of his thirty-nine-year regime led to its sometimes being called not only a *dictadura* (dictatorship) but also a *dictablanda* (a play on the words *dura* and *blanda*—"hard" and "soft", respectively—harking back to a usage that arose after Miguel Primo de Rivera's dictatorship ended in 1930).

FREEMASONS. See MASONS.

GENERALITAT. It has been the governing institution of Catalonia since the thirteenth century (with interruptions, including most recently during FRANCO's dictatorship).

GODED LLOPIS, MANUEL (1882–1936). He attempted suicide at the moment of his arrest, but his pistol failed to fire. At his court-martial he said that his rebellion was against anarchy, not the republican regime, citing as proof the fact that the rebels took to the streets shouting "Long live Spain!" and "Long live the Republic!" His execution was carried out less than a month after the uprising.

GONZÁLEZ GONZÁLEZ, VALENTÍN, "El Campesino" (1904–1983). A COMMUNIST miner (but his nickname means "the Peasant"), González fought on the republican side in many of the most intense and important battles of the war, at the head of a brigade of militias. General Escobar's antipathy to him was shared by others, prompting El Campesino to write, in a book published in 1952, "I was not guilty of ugly things myself, I never caused needless sacrifice of human lives. I am a Spaniard. We look upon life as tragic. We despise death." Beevor describes these statements as "not merely a grotesque self-indulgence, they are profoundly misleading." At the end of the war González went into exile in the Soviet Union, where for a time he was imprisoned in a labor camp. He then lived in France until he returned to Spain after the FRANCO regime gave way to democracy in 1978, living in Madrid until his death.

HERNÁNDEZ SARAVIA, JUAN (1880–1962). He fled Spain to live in exile in France (where he was with AZAÑA during the latter's last hours), and then in Mexico until his death.

HOSPITALLER ORDER OF THE BROTHERS OF SAINT JOHN OF GOD. Founded in the 1530s, the order has hospitals all over the world.

IBARROLA ORUETA, JUAN (1900–1976). He supported CASADO and BESTEIRO's coup against NEGRÍN and was in Alicante when the war ended. Arrested and court-martialed by the nationalists, Ibarrola was given a death sentence that was commuted to thirty years in prison. Released in the general amnesty at the end of World War II, he returned to his home in the Basque Country and lived out his life there.

IGLESIAS POSSE, PABLO (1850–1925). Founder of the SOCIALIST PARTY in 1879 and the UGT in 1888.

INTERNATIONAL BRIGADES. These were units of mostly young foreign volunteers (many of them COMMUNISTS) who fought on the republican side, recruited from some fifty countries and organized and directed by the Comintern. Totaling a maximum of twenty thousand volunteers at any one time, they were withdrawn from Spain in November 1938 in a bid by NEGRÍN for British and French support. Hemingway immortalized the International Brigades in his novel *For Whom the Bell Tolls.*

JOHN OF THE CROSS, SAINT (1542–1591). A great Spanish mystic and Doctor of the Church whose lyrical, rigorously intellectual poems are considered the summit of mystical Spanish literature.

JURADO BARRIO, ENRIQUE (1882–1965). A veteran of thirty years in the army when the war ended, Jurado's exile took him to France, Argentina, and Uruguay. He died in Montevideo.

LARGO CABALLERO, FRANCISCO (1869–1946). A plasterer who became president of the SOCIALIST PARTY and was prime minister of the REPUBLIC from September 1936 to May 1937, he fled to France at the end of the war. He was interned in a Nazi concentration camp until 1945, and he returned to France when he was freed at the end of World War II.

LARRAZÁBAL SALAS, RAMÓN (1916–1993). Nationalist colonel best known as the author of *History of the People's Army of the Republic* (Madrid, 1973).

LEGION (full name in Spanish: La Legión Española; in English: the Spanish Legion). Founded by ALFONSO XIII in 1920, it was and remains an elite corps within the Spanish army, with the battle cry *¡Viva la muerte!* (Long live death!). Beevor says it was composed in large part of fugitives and criminals, indoctrinated with a cult of virility and slaughter.

LISTER FORJÁN, ENRIQUE (1907–1994). A COMMUNIST republican general who studied at a Soviet military academy before the war, he fled to Moscow at the end of it. After a varied career that included serving as a general in the Red Army and the Yugoslav People's Army, he returned to Spain in 1977 but continued his activities as a Communist. He died in Madrid. See also MODESTO.

LLANO DE LA ENCOMIENDA, FRANCISCO (1877–1963). A graduate of the Infantry Academy in Toledo at seventeen, he remained loyal to the REPUBLIC and was the commanding republican general in Catalonia at the beginning of the war. He was arrested by GODED in Barcelona before Goded himself was arrested. When Goded said he felt abandoned by his comrades, Llano de la Encomienda replied, "Defeated, which isn't the same thing, Goded." Llano de la Encomienda had a lackluster record in the rest of the war, and when it ended he fled to France and then Mexico. He died in Mexico City.

MARAÑÓN Y POSADILLO, GREGORIO (1887–1960). A brilliant intellectual, humanist, and doctor of medicine specializing in endocrinology, he spent the war in Paris and returned to Madrid in 1943, where he lived until his death.

MASONS OR FREEMASONS. A fraternal order with roots going back at least as far as fifteenth-century Scotland that emerged as an important anticlerical force in European intellectual, cultural, and political life beginning in the Enlightenment of the eighteenth century. It generally fostered the kind of liberal thinking (in the classic sense of the word "liberal": favoring individual liberty, free trade, and moderate political and social reform) on which Western democracy is based. Because of its blood oath, Freemasonry has been met with opposition from the Roman Catholic Church or various arms of it (such as the Jesuits), and FRANCO set himself to suppressing it in Spain entirely by making it illegal and subject to severe punishment.

MATALLANA GÓMEZ, MANUEL (1894–1952). Matallana did not mince words at the Los Llanos meeting when NEGRÍN asked his opinion about continuing the war: "The people and the army agree on the necessity of ending the war immediately," Matallana said, giving more than a dozen detailed reasons in the starkest terms. Court-martialed by the nationalists after the war, Matallana was sentenced to twelve years in prison, from which he was released early. He spent the last years of his life in Madrid supporting his family by working as a construction crew foreman.

MENÉNDEZ PIDAL, RAMÓN (1869–1968). A philologist, historian, and director of the *Real Academia Española* (Royal Spanish Academy), he left Spain when the war broke out and returned when it was over. He died in Madrid.

MERA SANZ, CIPRIANO (1897–1975). He supported CASADO and BESTEIRO's coup against NEGRÍN and the COMMUNISTS at the end of the war, then went into exile in Oran and Casablanca. He was extradited to Spain in 1942 and condemned to death the next year; his sentence was changed to thirty years in prison and he was freed in 1946. He worked as a bricklayer in Paris until his death there.

MIAJA MENANT, JOSÉ (1878–1958). A graduate of the Infantry Academy in Toledo, he was a career soldier who served as the war's first republican minister of defense. He ended the war as head of the NATIONAL DEFENSE COUNCIL and went into exile in Algeria, France, and Mexico.

MODESTO GUILLOTO LEÓN, JUAN (1906–1969). A COMMUNIST who participated in many of the war's most important engagements, he was promoted to general in command of the Army of the Center less than a month before war's end. Beevor names him and LISTER as examples of the "new breed of republican commander [who] was young, aggressive, ruthless and personally brave" but suffered from a "rigidly traditional approach to tactics" and "military formality". Four days after his promotion to general, Modesto left Spain for exile in the Soviet Union, ultimately dying in Prague.

MOLA VIDAL, EMILIO (1887–1937). It was Mola who coined the term "fifth column", referring to nationalist sympathizers in Madrid who could be counted on to undermine the REPUBLIC from within as Mola's four columns of troops advanced on the city. He died on June 3, 1937, when his airplane crashed in bad weather.

MONARCHISTS (Alfonsine). Conservatives who supported the restoration of the Borbón royal line that descended from Fernando VII through his daughter Isabel II. The last member of that line to have occupied the throne before the war was ALFONSO XIII. Isabel's elevation to the throne (and therefore that of her descendants) was disputed by the CARLISTS on the ground that it could not pass to a female, so Fernando's brother Don Carlos should have inherited it upon the former's death.

MONTSENY MAÑÉ, FEDERICA (1905–1994). The daughter of ANARCHISTS and a lifelong anarchist intellectual, writer, activist, and leader, she was the first female cabinet minister (as minister of health in LARGO CABALLERO's republican government) in Spanish history. She condemned the Red Terror of the summer and fall of 1936 as "a lust for blood inconceivable in honest men before". Fleeing to France with her family in January 1939, she lived in exile there until returning to Spain in 1977. She died in Toulouse.

MORIONES Y LARRAGA, DOMINGO (1883–1964). Third Marquess of Oroquieta, Moriones was relieved by CASADO of his command of the Army of Andalusia after the latter's coup against NEGRÍN in the last stages of the war. Moriones' replacement was shot by the nationalists after the war. Moriones himself was sentenced to a prison term of ten years.

NATIONAL DEFENSE COUNCIL (in Spanish: Junta Nacional de Defensa). After their coup against NEGRÍN near the end of the war, CASADO and BESTEIRO established this council to govern the REPUBLIC and to negotiate peace with FRANCO on less than crushing terms. Franco insisted on unconditional surrender.

NATIONAL MOVEMENT (or just the MOVEMENT). The political party forged by FRANCO in April 1937 by merging the CARLISTS, CEDA, and the Alfonsine MONARCHISTS into the FALANGE. It was from then on the sole legal political party—in the nationalist zone during the war and thereafter anywhere in Spain—throughout Franco's rule.

NATIONAL REPUBLICAN GUARD. The CIVIL GUARD, after its metamorphosis and renaming by the republican government in August 1936.

NEGRÍN Y LÓPEZ, JUAN (1894–1946). Born to a prosperous family, he entered politics in 1929 and was elected to the CORTES as a Socialist in 1931. Early in the war, as finance minister of the REPUBLIC, he initiated the shipment of most of Spain's gold reserves to the Soviet Union for safekeeping. He relied heavily on COMMUNIST support as prime minister during the last two years of the war, which ultimately alienated many of his government's supporters. After CASADO and BESTEIRO'S coup Negrín fled to France, from which, after the Nazi occupation, he moved on to Great Britain and the United States. He resigned as prime minister of the Republic in 1945, a year before he died in Paris.

ORGAZ YOLDI, LUIS (1881–1946). A nationalist general and committed MONARCHIST who, when FRANCO failed to restore the monarchy, agitated and conspired against him but ultimately decided not to pursue a coup attempt. Less than a year before Orgaz' death, Franco made him Chief of the General Staff.

OROQUIETA, MARQUESS OF. See MORIONES Y LARRAGA, DOMINGO.

ORTEGA Y GASSET, JOSÉ (1883–1955). He was a prominent Spanish academic and intellectual—an essayist and philosopher—who was a leader of the university strike of January 1931, which set the stage for the municipal elections that followed in April and drove ALFONSO XIII into exile. Ortega left Spain when the war began and did not return (from Buenos Aires) to Europe (Portugal) until 1942. He gradually resumed life in Spain starting in 1945, and he died in Madrid.

PASIONARIA, LA: Isidora Dolores Ibárruri Gómez (1895–1989). As a young woman she was a CARLIST Catholic, but she joined the PCE at the age of twenty-six and went on to become one of its leading figures. Payne says she was Stalin's favorite Spanish COMMUNIST. A deputy in the CORTES and an exceptionally gifted and charismatic speaker, she became famous for her cry of *¡No pasarán!* (They shall not pass!) during the battle for Madrid. She went into exile in the Soviet Union at the end of the war but retained her leadership position in the PCE. Returning to Spain two years after FRANCO's death, she was reelected as a deputy to the CORTES representing the same constituency she had represented before the war.

PCE. See COMMUNIST PARTY OF SPAIN.

PEOPLE'S TRIBUNALS. These were courts established by LARGO CABALLERO's government in the late summer and fall of 1936, to replace the regular judicial authorities who had resigned, fled, or been murdered, and to rein in the violence and disorder that prevailed during the Red Terror. The new tribunals were composed of fourteen delegates from the POPULAR FRONT and the CNT, with three members of the old judiciary.

POPULAR FRONT. The assortment of at least a half-dozen political parties (including most importantly the SOCIALIST PARTY and PCE) that came together in January 1936 to win the elections in the following February. They went on to govern the REPUBLIC during the war, in alliance with the ANARCHISTS, but they never succeeded in developing the unity that would perhaps have enabled them to win it.

POZAS PEREA, SEBASTIÁN (1876–1946). He attained the rank of general twenty years before the outbreak of the war, during which he served the REPUBLIC as minister of the interior, commander of the Army of the Center, and then commander of the Army of the East. At the end of the war he fled to Mexico, where he lived until his death seven years later.

PRIETO TUERO, INDALECIO (1883–1962). A long-time member of the CORTES for the SOCIALIST PARTY, he led the latter into the POPULAR FRONT but was at first excluded from the government. His rival LARGO CABALLERO appointed him minister of marine and air in 1936, and in 1937 he became minister of defense in NEGRÍN's government. Prieto's outspoken pessimism as the war ground on was fully justified (Beevor calls him "the Cassandra of the Republic") but set him at odds with the COMMUNISTS and NEGRÍN, who in March 1938 removed him from his defense post. Prieto left Spain for Mexico but continued to participate in republican politics with little success (his overall goal was to negotiate an agreement with FRANCO) and left politics altogether in 1950. He lived out his days in Mexico.

PRIMO DE RIVERA Y SÁENZ DE HEREDIA, JOSÉ ANTONIO (1903–

1936). He was the founder of the FALANGE and son of Miguel Primo de Rivera, Spain's dictator during the 1920s (see Translator's Introduction). General Escobar does not mention José Antonio in his diary, but his presence hovered over FRANCO and his regime throughout the latter's career during and after the war. Intellectually brilliant and charismatic in person and as an orator, Primo de Rivera was executed by the local republicans in Alicante on November 20, 1936, thirty-nine years to the day before Franco's death. There was little love lost, if any, between the two men, and had it not been for the former's death, he would very likely have been a rival to the latter (and the only plausible one) for nationalist leadership. As it was, by forming the MOVEMENT around the FALANGE and exalting Primo de Rivera as a martyr, Franco in effect co-opted his memory and assumed his mantle.

QUEIPO DE LLANO Y SIERRA, GONZALO (1875–1951). A FREEMASON and something of a loose cannon, the very tall Queipo de Llano had a contentious rivalry with the much shorter FRANCO. Queipo made a kind of cult of virility and openly mocked that of Franco, who had a high-pitched voice. (Queipo joined others in referring to him as "Paca", the nickname for the feminine form of Francisco, and described him as "fat-assed" for good measure.) Franco sidelined him shortly after the end of the war, and he died in his home base, Seville.

REPUBLIC. The government of Spain established when ALFONSO XIII left the country to go into exile April 1931.

RODRÍGUEZ GARCÍA, MELCHOR (1893–1972). Known as the

"Red Angel" for saving the lives of many prisoners in his custody, he had three stays in prison himself after he remained in Spain at war's end. Sentenced to twenty years for his role in it, he was released after four, thanks to the intervention of nationalists bearing witness to his heroically courageous acts. He worked as an insurance agent but was imprisoned twice more for his political activities. He died in Madrid.

RODRÍGUEZ SALAS, EUSEBIO (1885–?). A former railroad worker who lost an arm in an accident, he was at one time an ANARCHIST but then gravitated toward the COMMUNISTS. He had already survived an attempt by the anarchists on his life before the Telefónica episode, but his participation in it enraged them all the more. At the end of the war he fled to the Dominican Republic and then to Mexico.

ROJO LLUCH, VICENTE (1894–1966). Chief of staff of the REPUBLIC's armed forces, he honed his gifts for strategic thinking during the ten years (1922–1932) he taught at the Infantry Academy in Toledo, the most prestigious institution of military education in Spain, and then during the four years he taught at the Superior War School before the war broke out. He left Spain for France as the war was nearing its end, and later lived in Argentina from 1943 to 1956. Returning to Spain in 1957 on terms negotiated by nationalist military officers and Roman Catholic clergymen, he was court-martialed and sentenced to prison for thirty years, but the sentence was suspended and he was later pardoned. He died at his home in Madrid.

ROMERALES QUINTERO, MANUEL (1875–1936). General Escobar says Romerales was shot during the night of the uprising itself, but in fact he was court-martialed a few weeks later, on August 26, and executed by a firing squad two days after that.

SAMBLANCAT Y SALANOVA, ÁNGEL (1885–1963). An ANARCHO-SYNDICALIST who was elected to the CORTES at the beginning of the REPUBLIC, and a prolific writer, editor, and translator (he is said to have worked in nine languages), as well as a lawyer, Samblancat went into exile after the war and continued to publish for the rest of his life. He died in Mexico.

SISTERS OF ADORATION (full name in Spanish: Adoratrices: Esclavas del Santísimo Sacramento y de la Caridad; in English: Adorers: Servants of the Blessed Sacrament and of Charity). An order of Roman Catholic nuns founded in 1856 in Madrid, it is engaged in social work in twenty-two countries, generally on behalf of sexually exploited women.

SOCIALIST PARTY (full name in Spanish: Partido Socialista Obrero de España, generally known by its initials the PSOE; in English: Spanish Socialist Workers Party). The PSOE is a left-of-center political party with nineteenth-century Marxist roots. Together with the PCE, it was an essential part of the coalition supporting the republican government during the war. Banned during the FRANCO years, it has since governed Spain twice (1982–1996 and 2004–2012) and is today its main opposition party.

SYNDICALISTS. See ANARCHISTS, ANARCHO-SYNDICALISTS.

TAGÜEÑA CORTE, MANUEL (1913–1971). He was a SOCIALIST at the start of the war but joined the PCE within a few months. Rising to colonel, he participated in many of the most important engagements of the war. He made his escape from Spain to France as the war was ending and then went to Mexico, where he spent the rest of his life in exile.

TARRADELLAS I JOAN, JOSEP (1899–1988). A lifelong politician who was a leading member of the Republican Left Party of Catalonia, he was a deputy of the CORTES in the early years of the REPUBLIC and occupied many posts in the cabinet of the GENERALITAT, including president and (at various times) counselor of finance, governance, culture, economy, and public services. He went into exile after the war, but he ultimately returned to Catalonia and negotiated the reestablishment of the Generalitat after FRANCO's death. He was made a marquess in 1986.

TORAL AZCONA, NILAMÓN (?–1983). A republican lieutenant colonel in command of the Toral Group (the equivalent of an army corps, but made up of various militia units), he was a COMMUNIST ex-boxer and businessman who held the rank of corporal when the war began. He is esteemed by RAMÓN SALAS LARRAZÁBAL as one of the three or four most capable leaders of the republican militias.

TRUETA I RASPALL, JOSEP (1897–1977). A medical doctor and surgeon in Barcelona during the war, he went into exile afterward in the United Kingdom, participating in the development of penicillin and becoming professor of orthopaedics at the University of Oxford. He retired and returned to Catalonia in 1966. When he died, a tribute to him in the *Journal of Bone and Joint Surgery* described his arrival in the United Kingdom as "a godsend".

UGT (full name in Spanish: Unión General de Trabajadores; in English: General Union of Workers). One of Spain's largest labor unions, during the war and also today, it was and is affiliated with the SOCIALIST PARTY.

VARELA IGLESIAS, JOSÉ ENRIQUE (1891–1951). A nationalist general and a CARLIST, after the war he served as minister of war, high commissioner of Spanish Morocco, and captain general of Madrid.

VIDAL Y BARRAQUER, FRANCISCO DE ASÍS (1868–1943). Cardinal and archbishop of Tarragona, he refused to sign the July 1, 1937, collective pastoral letter of the Catholic Church hierarchy in Spain expressing support for the nationalists' uprising. He spent the war in exile and died in Switzerland, never having returned to Spain.

YAGÜE Y BLANCO, JUAN (1891–1952). Nationalist general often called the "Butcher of Badajoz" for having ordered the massacre in the bullring there, in August 1936, of many men, women, and children (up to four thousand, by some estimates). Beevor says he was "undoubtedly the nationalists' most capable field commander". Commander of the LEGION during the war (as his military academy classmate FRANCO had been before him), FRANCO made him his minister of air after the war ended.

SOURCES

In addition to material available on the Internet (including the *Encyclopaedia Britannica* and *Wikipedia*), sources consulted include:

Arasa, Daniel. *Entre la cruz y la República: Vida y muerte del general Escobar*. Barcelona: Styria de Ediciones y Publicaciones, S.L., 2006.

Beevor, Antony. *The Battle for Spain: The Spanish Civil War 1936–1939*. London: Weidenfeld and Nicolson, 2006.

Payne, Stanley G. *The Franco Regime 1936–1975*. Madison: University of Wisconsin Press, 1987.

———. *Spain: A Unique History*. Madison: University of Wisconsin Press, 2011.

———. *The Spanish Civil War*. New York: Cambridge University Press, 2012.

Preston, Paul. *El gran manipulador: La mentira cotidiana de Franco*. Barcelona: Ediciones B, S.A., 2008.

———. *The Spanish Holocaust: Inquisition and Extermination in Twentieth-Century Spain*. New York and London: W. W. Norton and Company, 2012.

Thomas, Hugh. *The Spanish Civil War*. New York: The Modern Library, 2001.